THE
WEALTHY GREEK'S
CONTRACT WIFE

BY
PENNY JORDAN

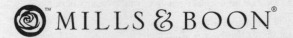

MILLS & BOON®

All the characters in this book have no existence outside the imagination of the author, and have no relation whatsoever to anyone bearing the same name or names. They are not even distantly inspired by any individual known or unknown to the author, and all the incidents are pure invention.

All Rights Reserved including the right of reproduction in whole or in part in any form. This edition is published by arrangement with Harlequin Enterprises II BV/S.à.r.l. The text of this publication or any part thereof may not be reproduced or transmitted in any form or by any means, electronic or mechanical, including photocopying, recording, storage in an information retrieval system, or otherwise, without the written permission of the publisher.

This book is sold subject to the condition that it shall not, by way of trade or otherwise, be lent, resold, hired out or otherwise circulated without the prior consent of the publisher in any form of binding or cover other than that in which it is published and without a similar condition including this condition being imposed on the subsequent purchaser.

® and ™ are trademarks owned and used by the trademark owner and/or its licensee. Trademarks marked with ® are registered with the United Kingdom Patent Office and/or the Office for Harmonisation in the Internal Market and in other countries.

First published in Great Britain 2009
Paperback edition 2010
Harlequin Mills & Boon Limited,
Eton House, 18-24 Paradise Road, Richmond, Surrey TW9 1SR

© Penny Jordan 2009

ISBN: 978 0 263 87763 2

Set in Times Roman 10½ on 12¼ pt
01-0210-50390

Harlequin Mills & Boon policy is to use papers that are natural, renewable and recyclable products and made from wood grown in sustainable forests. The logging and manufacturing process conform to the legal environmental regulations of the country of origin.

Printed and bound in Spain
by Litografia Rosés, S.A., Barcelona

Penny Jordan has been writing for more than twenty years and has an outstanding record: over 170 novels published, including the phenomenally successful A PERFECT FAMILY, TO LOVE, HONOUR AND BETRAY, THE PERFECT SINNER and POWER PLAY, which hit the *Sunday Times* and *New York Times* bestseller lists. Penny Jordan was born in Preston, Lancashire, and now lives in rural Cheshire.

Recent titles by the same author:

A BRIDE FOR HIS MAJESTY'S PLEASURE
THE SICILIAN BOSS'S MISTRESS*
THE SICILIAN'S BABY BARGAIN*
CAPTIVE AT THE SICILIAN BILLIONAIRE'S COMMAND*
TAKEN BY THE SHEIKH
THE SHEIKH'S BLACKMAILED MISTRESS
VIRGIN FOR THE BILLIONAIRE'S TAKING

The Leopardi Brothers

PROLOGUE

ILIOS MANOS looked out across the land that had belonged to his family for almost five centuries.

It was here on this rocky promontory, stretching out into the Aegean Sea in the north east of Greece, that Alexandros Manos had built for himself a copy of one of Palladio's most famous creations. Villa Emo.

Manos family folklore said that Alexandros Manos, a wealthy Greek merchant with his own fleet trading between Constantinople and Venice, had done business with the Emo family, and had been seized with envy for the new Emo mansion. He had secretly copied Palladio's drawings for the villa, taking them home to Greece with him, where he had had his own villa built, naming it Villa Manos and declaring that both it and the land on which it stood were a sacred trust, to be passed down from generation to generation, and must be owned by no man who was not of his blood.

It was here that Alexandros Manos had created what was in effect a personal fiefdom—a small kingdom of which he was absolute ruler.

Ilios knew that this promontory of land, surrounded on three sides by the Aegean Sea and with the mountains of northern Greece at its back, had meant everything to his grandfather, and Ilios's own father had given his life to keep it—just as his grandfather had forfeited his wealth to protect it. To protect *it*. But he hadn't protected the sons he had fathered, sacrificing them in order to keep his covenant with both the past and the future.

Ilios had learned a lot from his grandfather. He had learned that when you carried the hereditary responsibility of being descended from Alexandros Manos you had a duty to look beyond your own emotions—even to deny them if you had to—in order to ensure that the sacred living torch that was their family duty to the villa was passed on. The hand that carried that torch might be mortal, but the torch itself was for ever. Ilios had grown up listening to his grandfather's stories of what it meant to carry the blood of Alexandros Manos in your veins, and what it meant to be prepared to sacrifice anything and anyone to ensure that torch was passed on safely.

His was the duty to carry it now. And his too was the duty to do what his grandfather had not been able to do— and that was to restore their family's fortunes and its greatness.

As a boy, when Ilios had promised his grandfather that he would find a way to restore that greatness, his cousin Tino had laughed at him. Tino had laughed again when Ilios had told him that the only way he would pay off Tino's debts was if Tino sold him his half-share of their grandfather's estate to him.

Ilios looked at the building in front of him, the handsome face imprinted with the human history of so many generations of powerful self-willed men. It was set as though carved in marble by the same hands that had sculpted images of the Greek heroes of mythology. The golden eyes were a legacy of the wife Alexandros had brought back with him from northern lands, and they were fixed unwaveringly on the horizon.

Tino wasn't laughing any more. But he would be plotting to get his revenge, just as he had since their childhood. Tino had always wanted what little his cousin had, and would not take this humiliation lightly. As far as Tino was concerned, being born the son of a younger son was to labour under a disadvantage—something he blamed Ilios for.

Ilios knew the reputation he had amongst other men for striking a hard deal, and driving a hard bargain, for demanding the impossible from those who worked for him in order to create the impossible for those who paid him to do exactly that.

There was no black magic, no dark art, as some seemed to suppose in the means by which he had made his fortune in the construction business—other than that of determination and hard work, of endurance and driving himself to succeed. The graft that Ilios employed was not oiled by back-handers or grubby deals done in shadowed rooms, but by sheer hard work. By knowing his business inside out and from the bottom up—because that was where he himself had started. Even now, no commission that bore the name of Manos Construction did so until he had examined and passed every smallest detail. The pride and the sense of honour he took from his work, which he had inherited from his grandfather, saw to that.

Ilios knew that the journey he had made from the poverty of his childhood to the wealth that was now his filled other men with resentment and envy. It was said that no man could rise from penury to the wealth that Ilios possessed—counted in billions, not mere millions—by honest means alone, and he knew that few men envied him more, or would take more pleasure in his downfall, than his own cousin.

The rising sun struck across his profile, momentarily bathing it in bright gold reminiscent of the mask of the most famous of all of Greek Macedonians—Alexander the Great. He had been born in this part of Greece, and according to family lore had walked this very peninsula with his own forebears.

Several yards away from him one of his foremen waited, like the drivers of the heavy construction equipment behind him.

'What do you want me to do?' he asked.

Ilios gave the building in front of him a grim look.

'Destroy it. Pull it down and level the site.'

The foreman looked shocked.

'But your cousin—?'

'My cousin has no say in what happens here. Raze it to the ground.'

The foreman gave the signal to the drivers, and as the jaws of the heavy machinery bit into the building, reaching out to the morning sun, Ilios turned on his heel and walked away.

CHAPTER ONE

'So, what are you going to do, then?' Charley asked anxiously.

Lizzie looked at her younger sisters, the familiar need to protect them, no matter what the cost to herself, stiffening her resolve.

'There is only one thing I can do,' she answered. 'I shall have to go.'

'What? Fly out to Thessalonica?'

'It's the only way.'

'But we haven't got any money.'

That was Ruby, the baby of the family at twenty-two, sitting at the kitchen table while her five-year-old twin sons, who had been allowed a rare extra half an hour of television, sat uncharacteristically quietly in the other room, so that the sisters could discuss the problems threatening them.

No, they hadn't got any money—and that was her fault, Lizzie acknowledged guiltily.

Six years earlier, when their parents had died together, drowned by a freak wave whilst they were on holiday, Lizzie had promised herself that she would do everything she could to keep the family together. She had left university, and had been working for a prestigious London-based interior design partnership, in pursuit of her dream of getting a job as a set designer. Charley had just started university, and Ruby had been waiting to sit her GCSE exams.

Theirs had been a close and loving family, and the shock of losing their parents had been overwhelming—especially for Ruby, who, in her despair, had sought the love and reassurance she so desperately needed in the arms of the man who had abandoned her and left her pregnant with the adored twin boys.

There had been other shocks for them to face, though. Their handsome, wonderful father and their pretty, loving mother, who had created for them the almost fairytale world of happiness in which the family had lived, had done just that—lived in a fairytale which had little or no foundation in reality.

The beautiful Georgian rectory in the small Cheshire village in which they had grown up had been heavily mortgaged, their parents had not had any life insurance, and they had had large debts. In the end there had been no alternative but for their lovely family home to be sold, so those debts could be paid off.

With the property market booming, and her need to do everything she could to support and protect her sisters, Lizzie had used her small savings to set up in business on her own in an up-and-coming area south of Manchester— Charley would be able to continue with her studies at Manchester University, Ruby could have a fresh start, and she could establish a business which would support them all.

At first things had gone well. Lizzie had won contracts to model the interiors of several new building developments, and from that had come commissions from homebuyers to design the interiors of the properties they had bought. Off the back of that success Lizzie had taken the opportunity to buy a much larger house from one of the developers for whom she'd worked—with, of course, a much larger mortgage. It had seem to make sense at the time—after all, with the twins and the three of them they'd definitely needed the space, just as they had needed a large four-wheel drive vehicle. She used it to visit the sites on which she worked, and Ruby used it to take the boys to school. In addition to that her clients, a small local firm, had been pressuring her to buy, so that they could wind up the development and move on to a new site.

But then had come the credit crunch, and overnight almost everything had changed. The bottom had dropped out of the property market, meaning that they were unable to trade down and reduce the mortgage because of the value of the house had decreased so much, and with that of course Lizzie's commissions had dried up. The money she had been putting away in a special savings account had not increased anything like as much as she had expected, and financially things had suddenly become very dark indeed.

Right now Charley was still working as a project manager for a local firm, and Ruby had said that she would get a job. But neither Lizzie nor Charley wanted her to do that. They both wanted the twins to have a mother at home, just as they themselves had had. And, as Lizzie had said six months ago, when they'd first started to feel the effects of the credit crunch, she would get a job working for someone else, and she still had money owing to her from various clients. They would manage.

But it turned out she had been overly optimistic. She hadn't been able to get a job, because what industry there was in the area geared towards personal spending was shedding workers, and with the cost of basics going up they were now struggling to manage. They were only just about keeping their heads above water. Many of her clients had cancelled their contracts, and some of them still owed her large sums of money she suspected she would never receive.

In fact things were so dire that Lizzie had already made a private decision to go to the local supermarket and see if she could get work there. But then the letter had arrived, and now they—or rather *she* was in an even more desperate situation.

Two of her more recent clients, for whom she had done a good deal of work, had further commissioned her to do the interior design for a small block of apartments they had bought in northern Greece. On a beautiful promontory, the apartments were to have been the first stage in a luxurious and exclusive holiday development which, when finished, would include villas, three five-star hotels, a marina, restaurants and everything that went with it.

The client had given her carte blanche to furnish them in an 'upmarket Notting Hill style'.

Notting Hill might be a long way from their corner of industrialised Manchester, on the Cheshire border, but Lizzie had known exactly what her clients had meant: white walls, swish bathrooms and kitchens, shiny marble floors, glass furniture, exotic plants and flowers, squishy sofas…

Lizzie had flown out to see the apartments with her clients, a middle-aged couple whom she had never really been able to take to. She had been disappointed by the architectural design of the apartments. She had been expecting something creative and innovative that still fitted perfectly into the timeless landscape, but what she had seen had been jarringly out of place. A six-storey-high rectangular box of so-called 'duplex apartments', reached by a narrow track that forked into two, with one branch sealed off by bales of dangerous-looking barbed wire. Hardly the luxury holiday homes location she had been expecting.

But when she had voiced her doubts to her clients, suggesting that the apartments might be difficult to sell, they had assured her that she was worrying unnecessarily.

'Look, the fact is that we bargained the builder down to such a good price that we couldn't lose out even if we let the whole lot out for a tenner a week,' Basil Rainhill had joked cheerfully. At least Lizzie had assumed it as a joke. It was hard to tell with Basil at times.

He came from money, as his wife was fond of telling her. 'Born with a silver spoon in his mouth, and of course Basil has such an eye for a good investment. It's a gift, you know. It runs in his family.'

Only now the gift had run out. And just before the Rainhills themselves had done the same thing disappearing, leaving a mountain of debt behind them, Basil Rainhill had told Lizzie that, since he couldn't now afford to pay her bill, he was instead making over to her a twenty per cent interest in the Greek apartment block.

Lizzie would much rather have had the money she was owed, but her solicitor had advised her to accept, and so she had become a partner in the ownership of the apartments along with the Rainhills and Tino Manos, the Greek who owned the land.

Design-wise, she had done her best with the limited possibilities presented by the apartment block, sticking to her rule of sourcing furnishings as close to where she was working as possible, and she had been pleased with the final result. She'd even been cautiously keeping her fingers crossed that, though she suspected they wouldn't sell, when the whole complex was finished she might look forward to the apartments being let to holidaymakers and bringing her in some much-needed income.

But now she had received this worrying, threatening letter, from a man she had never heard of before, insisting that she fly out to Thessalonica to meet him. It stated that there were 'certain legal and financial matters with regard to your partnership with Basil Rainhill and my cousin Tino Manos which need to be resolved in person', and included the frighteningly ominous words, 'Failure to respond to this letter will result in an instruction to my solicitors to deal with matters on my behalf'. The letter had been signed *Ilios Manos*.

His summons couldn't have come at worse time, but the whole tone of Ilios Manos's letter was too threatening for Lizzie to feel she could refuse to obey it. As apprehensive and unwilling to meet him as she was, the needs of her family must come first. She had a responsibility to them, a duty of love from which she would never abdicate, no matter what the cost to herself. She had sworn that— promised it on the day of her parents' funeral.

'If this Greek wants to see you that badly he might at least have offered to pay your airfare,' Ruby grumbled.

Lizzie felt so guilty.

'It's all my own fault. I should have realised that the property market was over-inflated, and creating a bubble that would burst.'

'Lizzie, you mustn't blame yourself.' Charley tried to comfort her. 'And as for realising what was happening— how could you when governments didn't even know?'

Lizzie forced a small smile.

'Surely if you tell the bank why you need to go to Greece they'll give you a loan?' Ruby suggested hopefully.

Charley shook her head. 'The banks aren't giving any businesses loans at the moment. Not even successful ones.'

Lizzie bit her lip. Charley wasn't reproaching her for the failure of her business, she knew, but she still felt terrible. Her sisters relied on her. She was the eldest, the sensible one, the one the other two looked to. She prided herself on being able to take care of them—but it was a false pride, built on unstable foundations, as so much else in this current terrible financial climate.

'So what is poor Lizzie going to do? She's got this Greek threatening to take things further if she doesn't go and see him, but how can she if we haven't got any money?' Ruby asked their middle sister.

'We have,' Lizzie suddenly remembered, with grateful relief. 'We've got my bucket money, and I can stay in one of the apartments.'

Lizzie's 'bucket money' was the spare small change she had always put in the decorative tin bucket in her office, in the days when she had possessed 'spare' change.

Two minutes later they were all looking at the small tin bucket, which was now on the kitchen table.

'Do you think there'll be enough?' Ruby asked dubiously

There was only one way to find out.

'Eighty-nine pounds,' Lizzie announced half an hour later, when the change had been counted.

'Eighty-nine pounds and four pence,' Charley corrected her.

'Will it be enough?' Ruby asked.

'I shall make it enough,' Lizzie told them determinedly. It would certainly buy an off-season low-cost airline ticket, and she still had the keys for the apartments—apartments in which she held a twenty per cent interest. She was surely perfectly entitled to stay in one whilst she tried to sort out the mess the Rainhills had left behind.

How the mighty were fallen—or rather the not so mighty in her case, Lizzie reflected tiredly. All she had wanted to do was provide for her sisters and her nephews, to protect them and keep them safe financially, so that never ever again would they have to endure the truly awful spectre of repossession and destitution which had faced them after their parents' death.

CHAPTER TWO

No! It was impossible, surely! The apartment block *couldn't* simply have disappeared.

But it had.

Lizzie blinked and looked again, desperately hoping she was seeing things—or rather not seeing them—but it was no use. It still wasn't there.

The apartment block had gone.

Where she had expected to see the familiar rectangular building there was only roughly flattened earth, scarred by the tracks of heavy building plant.

It had been a long and uncomfortable ride, in a taxi driven at full pelt by a Greek driver who'd seemed bent on proving his machismo behind the wheel, after an equally lacking in comfort flight on the low-cost airline.

They had finally turned off the main highway to travel along the dusty, narrow and rutted unfinished road that ran down to the tip of the peninsula and the apartments. Whilst the taxi had bounded and rocked from side to side, Lizzie had braced herself against the uncomfortable movement, noticing as they passed it that where the road forked, and where last year there had been rolls of spiked barbed wire blocking the entrance to it, there were now imposing-looking padlocked wrought-iron gates.

The taxi driver had dropped her off when the ruts in the road had become so bad that he had refused to go any further. She had insisted on him giving her a price before they had left the airport, knowing how little money she had to spare, and before she handed it over to him she took from him a card with a telephone number on it, so that she could call for a taxi to take her into the city to meet Ilios Manos after she had settled herself into an apartment and made contact with him.

Lizzie stared at the scarred ground where the apartment block should have been, and then lifted her head, turning to look out over the headland, where the rough sparse grass met the still winter-grey of the Aegean. The brisk wind blowing in from the sea tasted of salt—or was the salt from her own wretched tears of shock and disbelief?

What on earth was going on? Basil had boasted to her that twenty per cent entitled her to two apartments, each worth two hundred thousand euros. Lizzie would have put the value closer to one hundred thousand, but it still meant that whatever value they'd potentially held had vanished— along with the building. It was money she simply could not afford to lose.

What on earth was she going to do? She had just under fifty euros in her purse, nowhere to stay, no immediate means of transport to take her back to the city, no apart- ments—nothing. Except, of course, for the threat implied in the letter she had received. She still had that to deal with—and the man who had made that threat.

To say that Ilios Manos was not in a good mood was to put it mildly, and, like Zeus, king of the gods himself, Ilios could make the atmosphere around him rumble with the threat of dire consequences to come when his anger was aroused. As it was now.

The present cause of his anger was his cousin Tino. Thwarted in his attempt to get money out of Ilios via his illegal use of their grandfather's land, he had now turned his attention to threatening to challenge Ilios's right of inheritance. He was claiming that it was implicit in the tone of their grandfather's will that Ilios should be married, since the estate must be passed down through the family, male to male. Of course Ilios knew this—just as he knew that ultimately he must provide an heir.

Ilios had been tempted to dismiss Tino's threat, but to his fury his lawyers had warned him that it might be better to avoid a potentially long drawn-out and costly legal battle and simply give Tino the money he wanted.

Give in to Tino's blackmail? *Never.* Ilios's mouth hardened with bitterness and pride.

Inside his head he could hear his lawyer's voice, saying apologetically, 'Well, in that case, then maybe you should think about finding yourself a wife.'

'Why, when Tino doesn't have anything resembling a proper case?' Ilios had demanded savagely.

'Because your cousin has nothing to lose and you have a very great deal. Your time and your money could end up being tied up for years in a complex legal battle.'

A battle which once engaged upon he would not be able to withdraw from unless and until he had won, Ilios acknowledged.

His lawyer had suggested he take some time to review the matter, perhaps hoping Ilios knew that he would give in and give Tino the one million euros he wanted—a small enough sum of money to a man who was, after all, a billionaire. But that wasn't the point. The point was that Tino thought that he could get the better of him by simply putting his hand out for money he hadn't earned. There was no way that Ilios was going to allow that.

He had been attempting to vent some of the fury he was feeling by felling branches from an old and diseased olive tree when he had seen a taxi come down the road to the headland, stopping to let its passenger get out before turning round and going back the way it had come.

Now, still wearing the old hard hat bearing the Manos Construction logo he had put on for protection, his arms bare in a white tee shirt, his jeans tucked into work boots, he walked out from the tree line and watched as Lizzie looked out to sea, his arms folded across his chest.

Lizzie turned back towards the flattened ground where the apartments had been, shock holding her immobile as she saw the man standing on it, watching her.

'You're trespassing. This is private land.'

He spoke English! But the words he had spoken were hostile and angry, challenging Lizzie to insist with equal hostility, 'Private land which in part belongs to me.'

It wasn't strictly true, of course, but as a partner in the apartment block she must surely own a percentage of the land on which it had been built? Lizzie didn't know the finer points of Greek property law, but there was something about the attitude toward her of the man confronting her and challenging her that made her feel she had to assert herself and her rights. However, it was plain that she had done the wrong thing. The man unfolded his arms, revealing the outline of a hard-muscled torso beneath the dirt-smeared tee shirt tucked into low-slung jeans that rode his hips, and strode towards her.

'Manos land can never belong to anyone other than a Manos.'

He was savagely angry. The hardness of the gaze from golden eagle eyes fringed with thick dark lashes speared her like a piece of helpless prey.

Lizzie stepped back from him in panic, and lost her footing as she stumbled on a rough tussock of grass.

As she started to fall the man reached for her, hard fingers biting into her jacket-clad arms as she was hauled upright and kept there by his hold on her. The golden gaze raked her with a predatory male boldness that infuriated her. He was looking at her as though…as though he was indeed a mythical Greek god, with the right and the power to take and use vulnerable female mortal flesh for his own pleasure as and when he wished. Sex with a man like this would be dangerous for the woman who was drawn to risk herself in his hostile embrace. Would he take without giving, or would he subjugate a woman foolish enough to think she could make him want her by overpowering her with his sensuality and leaving her a prisoner to it whilst he remained unmoved? That mouth, with its full bottom lip, suggested that he possessed a cruel sensuality that matched his manner towards her.

Lizzie shivered, shocked by the inappropriateness and the unfamiliar sensuality of her own thoughts. She tried to concentrate on something practical.

Somehow as he'd moved he'd also found time to push back the protective hard hat he was wearing, so that now she could see the thick darkness of his hair. She was five foot six. He was much taller—well over six foot—and of course far more powerful that her. Lizzie could see that the effort of holding her had hardly raised the biceps in his powerful arms, but that didn't stop her from trying break free of him.

He stopped her with contemptuous ease, pulling her closer to him. He smelled of earth, and hard work, and of being a man. From somewhere deep down, in the place where she kept her most special memories, she had a sudden mental image of being held in her father's arms in the garden at her parents' lovely house in Cheshire, laughing in delight as she looked down from that height to where her mother was kneeling beside her two younger sisters. Those had been such wonderful years—years when she had felt safe and secure and loved.

But this man was not her father. With this man there would be no safety, no security, and certainly no love.

Love? She was so close to the dirt-streaked tee shirt that she could see the dark shadow of his body hair through it. She could almost feel the force of his hostility towards her. And she felt equally hostile to him. That was why her heart was banging into her chest wall and why her senses were recoiling from the intense awareness of him that his proximity was forcing on her.

What kind of awareness? Awareness of him as a man? Awareness of his maleness? Awareness of his sexuality? Awareness that within her something long denied, something starved of the right to express itself, was pushing against the barriers she had erected against it. Because of this man?

No, of course not. That was impossible. Her heart was thudding even more frantically, pumping adrenalin-fuelled denial through her veins. Why was she reacting to him like this? She had no interest in his sexuality. She *must not* have any interest in his sexuality. She must not want to stay here in his arms.

The panic caused by her own feelings had Lizzie demanding fiercely, 'Let go of me.'

Ilios wasn't used to women demanding to be set free when he was holding them—quite the opposite. Normally women—especially women like he knew this one to be: selfish, shallow, self-seeking women who cared nothing for others—were all too keen to inveigle themselves into situations of intimacy with him. Which was, of course, why he felt so reluctant to release her.

When she pulled back against him the movement of her body released the scent she was wearing, delicate and light. Deep down inside him something visceral and unfamiliar jerked into hot molten life. Desire? For a woman like this? Impossible. He released her abruptly, stepping back from her.

'Who are you?' Lizzie asked unsteadily, struggling for balance both physically and emotionally.

'Ilios Manos,' Ilios told her curtly.

This man was Ilios Manos? The man who had sent her that letter? Lizzie's heart thumped into her ribs, its sledge-hammer blow fired by shock.

'Ilios Manos, the owner of this land on which you have no right to be, Miss Wareham,' Ilios told her grimly.

'How do you know who I am?' The question had been spoken before Lizzie could stop herself.

'Your name is on your suitcase strap,' Ilios pointed out curtly, gesturing towards the brightly coloured strap wrapped around the handle of the small trolley case she had abandoned in the shock of discovering that the apartment block had gone.

'What's happened to the apartments?'

'I gave orders for them to be knocked down.'

'What? Why? You had no right.' Her shocked disbelief deepened her anger, and also in some illogical way her awareness of him—as though she had developed some unwanted new sense designed exclusively to register everything about him and make her intensely receptive to that information. From the way the narrowing of his eyes fanned out fine lines around his eyes to the shape of his mouth as he spoke and her extreme awareness of the powerful maleness of his body.

'I had every right. They were on my land. Illegally on my land.'

Lizzie struggled to clamp down on her awareness of him.

'The land belongs to my partner, Tino Manos, not you.'

'My cousin has ceded his right to the land to me.'

'But you can't just knock down a block of apartments like that. Apart from anything else, two of them belonged to me.'

'Yes,' he agreed, 'they did.'

There was something about the way he was looking at her that made Lizzie feel extremely uneasy—as though she had unwittingly stepped into some kind of trap.

'Tell me, Miss Wareham, what kind of greed makes a person ignore the normal rules of law to grab at something even when they know it must be fraudulent?' His voice was deeply cynical, his whole manner towards her menacing and iced with bitter contempt.

'I…I don't know what you're talking about.' Lizzie protested truthfully.

'Of course you do. You were in partnership with my cousin. You have said so yourself. You must have known about the building regulations that were broken, about the suppliers and workmen left unpaid in order to build the apartments at a minimum cost to your partnership, and for the maximum ultimate profit.'

'No, I didn't,' Lizzie insisted. But she could see that he didn't believe her.

'Have you any idea of the damage your greed has caused? The hardship it has inflicted on those you cheated?

Or do you simply not care? Well, I intend to make sure that you *do* care, Miss Wareham. I will make sure that you pay back everything you owe.'

Ilios was angrier than he could ever remember being. His cousin had systematically tried to cheat him and manipulate him at every turn, and now Tino was even daring to challenge his legitimacy to what was rightfully his. Ilios could feel his fury boiling up inside him. His cousin might not be here to pay for what he had done, but his partner in crime, this Englishwoman who actually dared to lie to him, *was* here, and she would bear the brunt of his fury and his retribution, Ilios decided savagely.

'Everything I owe?' Lizzie objected, her heart sinking. 'What do you mean? I don't owe anybody anything.'

Her determination to continue lying to him hardened Ilios's resolve to inflict retribution on her. She was everything he most disliked and despised in her sex. Dishonest, and attempting to cloak her dishonesty with an air of pseudo-innocence that manifested itself in the way she was dressed—simply, in jeans worn with a tee shirt and a plain jacket—and in her face with its admittedly beautiful bone structure, free of make-up.

Just as that damn elusive scent she was wearing had made him want to draw her closer, to pursue it and capture it, so the pink lipstick that deliberately drew his attention to the fullness of her mouth made him want to capture her lips to see if they were as soft as they looked. Where another less skilled woman might have tried to use artifice to mask her deceit, Elizabeth Wareham used art—the art of appearing modest, honest, vulnerable. Well, it wouldn't work on him. Anyone who did business with his cousin had to be as dishonest and scheming as manipulative as Tino was himself. Like attracted like, after all. She could try using her sexuality to disarm him as much as she liked. He wasn't going to be taken in.

When Ilios Manos didn't respond, Lizzie stiffened her spine and her resolve and repeated, as firmly as she could, 'I don't owe anyone in Greece any money, and I don't understand why you think I do.'

'I don't *think* you do, Miss Wareham. I know you do—because the person you owe money to is me.'

Lizzie gulped in air and tried not to panic. 'But that's not possible.'

Ilios was in no mood to let her continue lying to him. 'You owe me money, Miss Wareham, because of your involvement with the apartments built by my cousin on my land. Plus there is also the matter of the outstanding payments for goods and services provided by local suppliers to you.'

'That isn't my fault. The Rainhills were supposed to pay them,' Lizzie defended herself.

'The contract supplied to me by my cousin states unequivocally that *you* are to pay them.'

'No—that can't be possible,' Lizzie repeated

'I assure you that it is.'

'I have my copy of the contract here with me, and it states quite plainly that the owners of the apartments are to pay the suppliers direct,' Lizzie insisted.

'Contracts can be altered.'

'And in this case they obviously have been—but not by me.' Lizzie's face was burning with disbelief and despair.

'And you can prove this?' Ilios Manos was demanding, the expression on his face making it plain that he did not believe her.

'I have a contract that states that my *clients* are responsible for paying the suppliers.'

'That is not what I asked you. The contract I have states unequivocally that *you* are responsible for paying them. And then there is the not so small matter of your share of the cost of taking down the apartments and returning the land to its original state.'

'Taking down the apartments?' Lizzie echoed. 'But that was nothing to do with me. You were the one who ordered their destruction—you told me that yourself...'

Lizzie badly wanted to sit down. She was tired and shocked and frightened, but she knew she couldn't show those weaknesses in front of this stone-faced man who looked like a Greek god but spoke to her as cruelly as Hades himself, intent on her destruction. She was sure he would never show any sign of human weaknesses himself, or make any allowances for those who possessed them. But there was nowhere to sit, nowhere to hide, to escape from the man now watching her with such determined intention on breaking her on the wheel of his anger.

'I had no choice. Even if I had wanted to keep them it would have been impossible, given their lack of sound construction. The truth is that they were a death trap. A death trap on *my* land, masquerading as a building constructed by *my* company.'

As he spoke Ilios remembered how he had felt on learning how his cousin had tried to use the good name of the business Ilios had built up quite literally with his own bare hands for his nefarious purposes, and his anger intensified.

His company. Lizzie automatically looked at his hard hat and its logo. She remembered Basil Rainhill smirking when he'd told her that Manos construction was 'fronting' the building of the apartments, and that they had a first-class reputation. Then she had assumed his smirk was because of the good deal he has boasted about to her, but now…

'I don't know anything about how the apartments were built. In fact, I don't understand what this is about. I was contracted to design the interiors of the apartments, that's all.'

'Oh, come, Miss Wareham—do you really expect me to believe that when I have a contract that states unequivocally that payment for your work was to be a twenty per cent interest in the apartment block?'

'That was only because the Rainhills couldn't pay me. They offered me that in lieu of my fee.'

'I am not remotely interested in how you came by your share in the illegal construction my cousin built on my land, only that you pay your share of the cost of making good the damage as well as what you owe your suppliers.'

'You're making this up,' Lizzie protested.

'*You* are daring to call *me* a liar?' Ilios grabbed hold of her, gripping her arms as he had done before. How had she dared to accuse him of lying? His desire to punish her, to force her to take back her accusation, to kiss her until the only sound to come from her lips was a soft moan of surrender, pounded through him, crashing through the barriers of civilized behaviour and forcing him to fight for his self-control.

She had said the wrong thing, Lizzie knew. Ilios Manos was not the man to accuse of lying. His pride lay across his features like a brand, informing every expression that crossed his face—and, Lizzie suspected, every thought that entered his head.

He was still holding her, and his touch burned her flesh like a small electrical shock. Her chest lifted with her protesting intake of air. Immediately his gaze dropped to her body with predatory swiftness—as though somehow he knew that when he had touched her, her flesh had responded to his touch in a way that had flung her headlong into a place she didn't know, brought her face to face with a Lizzie she didn't know. Her heart was thumping jerkily, her senses intensely aware of him, and her gaze was drawn to him as though he was a magnet, clinging to his torso, his throat, his mouth.

She swung dizzily and helplessly between disbelief and a craving to move closer to him. Beneath her clothes her breasts swelled and ached, in response to a mastery she was powerless to resist. How could this be happening to her? How could her body be reacting to Ilios Manos as though…as though it *wanted* him? It must be some weird form of shock, Lizzie decided shakily as he released her, almost thrusting her away from him.

'I'm not calling you a liar,' Lizzie denied, feeling obliged to backtrack, if only to remind herself of the reality of her situation. 'I'm just saying that I think you've got some of your facts wrong. And besides—why aren't you demanding recompense from your cousin, instead of threatening and bullying me?' she demanded, quickly going on the attack.

Attack was, after all, the best form of defence, so they said, and she certainly needed to defend herself against what she had felt when he had held her. How could that have happened? She simply wasn't like that. She couldn't be. She had her family to think of. Being sexually aroused by a man she had only just met, a man who despised and disliked her, just wasn't the kind of thing she had ever imagined being. Not ever, and certainly not now.

Determinedly she martialled her scattered thoughts and pointed out, 'After all, I only owned twenty per cent of the apartment block. Your cousin, from what the Rainhills told me, owned the land, most of the apartments and was responsible for the building work. I never even met him, never mind discussed his business plan with him. I was given the apartments and made a partner in lieu of payment for the work I'd done. That's all.'

Ilios knew that that was true, but right now it didn't suit his mood to allow her any escape route—especially now that his cousin had increased his fury by continuing to plot against him. Ilios wanted repayment, he wanted retribution, he wanted vengeance—and he would have them. Ilios hated cheats, and he hated even more being forced to let them get away with cheating.

'My cousin has no assets and is heavily in debt. The Rainhills, as I am sure you have discovered yourself, have disappeared. And, whilst you might only own twenty per cent of the apartment block's value, the partnership agreement you signed contains what is called a joint and several guarantee—which means that each partner is both jointly and severally liable for the debts of the whole partnership. That means that I can claim from you recompense for the entire amount owing.'

'No, that can't be true,' Lizzie protested, horrified.

Ilios looked at her. There was real panic in her voice now. He could see that she was trembling.

An act, he told himself grimly. That was all it was. Just an act.

'I assure you that it is,' he told her, ignoring her obvious distress.

'But I can't possibly find that kind of money.' She couldn't find *any* kind of money.

'No? Well, I have to tell you that I intend to be fully recompensed—not just for the money I am owed, but also for the potential damage that could have been done to my business. A business for which I have worked far harder than someone like you, who lives off the naïveté of others, can ever imagine. You own your own business?'

'Yes,' Lizzie acknowledged. 'But it is almost bankrupt.'

Why had she told him that when she hadn't even told her sisters just how bad things were? That every spare penny she had had been placed into their shared joint account to ensure that the mortgage was paid, the household bills met, and food put on the table at home.

She looked really distraught now, Ilios could see, but he refused to feel any sympathy. Showing sympathy was a sign of weakness, and Ilios never allowed himself to be weak.

'You have a property? A home, I assume?' he pressed

'Yes, but it is mortgaged, and anyway I share it with my sisters, one of whom has two small children and is dependent on me.'

Lizzie didn't know why she was admitting all of this to him, other than because she was in such a state of shock and panic. She wasn't going to let herself think about the last few months of long nights, when she had lain awake worrying about how she would manage to protect her family and continue to provide for them financially. They knew that things were bad, she hadn't been able to hide that from them, but they did not know yet just how bad.

'Your sister does not have a husband to support her and her children? You do not have parents?'

'The answer to both those questions is no. Not that it is any of your business, or relevant to our discussion. There is no way I can find the money to repay you. The only thing I own that is my own is my body…'

'And you wish to offer *that* to me in payment?'

Lizzie was horrified.

'No! Never!'

Her immediate recoil, coupled with her vehemence, inflamed Ilios even further. Was she daring to suggest that she was too good for him? Morally superior to him? Well, he would soon make her change her tune, Ilios promised himself savagely.

'You deny it now, but the offer was implicit in your declaration that your body is the only thing you have.'

He was determined to humiliate her. Lizzie could see that. Because he had somehow sensed her sexual reaction to him?

'No. That is, yes—but I didn't mean it the way you are trying to suggest. I only meant that I do not own anything via which I could raise the money to pay you.'

'Except your body.'

'I didn't mean it like that,' Lizzie repeated, mortified. 'I just meant that…' She lifted her hand to her head, which was now pounding with a mixture of anxiety and despair. 'I can't pay you.'

Ilios had had enough. His temper was at breaking point. He would have what he was owed—one way or another.

'Very well, then,' he began, causing Lizzie to go weak with relief at the thought that he was finally going to accept that there was no point in him continuing to press her for money.

'If your body is all you have with which to repay me, then that is what I will have to take—because I promise you this: I *will* have repayment.'

CHAPTER THREE

LIZZIE'S head jerked back on the slender stem of her neck as she looked up at Ilios in shocked disbelief.

'You—you can't mean that!' she protested. But even as she protested, something fierce and elemental was flaring up inside her—a desire, an excitement, a wild surge of female longing that shook her body with its force and shamed her pride with what it said about her. She couldn't want him—and most especially she could not want him under circumstances that should have been making her recoil with revulsion.

'I do mean it,' Ilios assured her.

'I can't believe that anyone could be so...cruel and inhuman, so lacking in compassion or understanding.'

The sudden explosion of sound from Lizzie's mobile phone, announcing the arrival of a text message, momentarily distracted them both.

Watching the way Lizzie reached frantically for her mobile to read it, Ilios gave her a look of cold contempt.

'You are obviously eager to read your lover's message, but—'

'It's from my sisters,' Lizzie interrupted him abstractedly, without lifting her gaze from the small screen. 'Wanting to know if everything is all right.'

'And you, of course, are going to reply and tell them all about the my so called cruelty and inhumanity.'

'No,' Lizzie told him. 'If I did they'd worry about me, and that's the last thing I want. I'm the eldest. It's my job to look after them and protect them. Not the other way around.'

Ilios digested her response in silence. An eldest sister determined to protect her younger siblings wasn't the way he wanted to think about this woman.

'The light's fading,' he told her, gesturing towards the horizon where the winter sun, half obscured by clouds, was starting to dip below the horizon. 'Soon it will be dark. I have to return to Thessaloniki. We can continue our discussion there.'

Over her dead body, Lizzie thought rebelliously, suddenly seeing an opportunity to put some much needed distance between them. She hated the thought of running away instead of staying to fight and prove her innocence, but with a man like this one, hell-bent on extracting payment from her—in kind if he could not have cash—the normal rules of engagement didn't seem the best course of action.

'Very well,' she agreed, reaching for her mobile again.

'What are you doing?' Ilios demanded.

'Telephoning for a taxi,' Lizzie answered.

Ilios shook his head. 'There's no point. You won't get one to come all the way out here—and anyway it isn't necessary. You can travel back with me.'

'No! I mean, no, thank you. I prefer to make my own arrangements,' Lizzie insisted, whilst her heartbeat raced in panicky dread in case he guessed that the reason she was so reluctant to travel with him was not that she was afraid of the intimacy between them it would entail, but that she was afraid a part of her might actually welcome that intimacy.

'You can drop the prim stance,' Ilios told her. 'I can assure you that I have no intention of using my car as a makeshift brothel—and besides, the amount you owe me would require far more in repayment than a single fumble in the back of a car.'

As he finished speaking Ilios reached for Lizzie's trolley case, his swift possession of it leaving her with no option other than to nod her head in unwilling acceptance of his offer.

'This way,' Ilios commanded.

He had walked over the headland from Villa Manos, and it would be easier to walk back there rather than him leaving Lizzie here whilst he went for the car. And besides, he didn't trust her not to try to cheat him a second time by attempting to leave without paying her debt.

The path was narrow and single track, climbing over the headland, and Ilios was making it plain that he expected her to go first, Lizzie could see. In normal circumstances she would have enjoyed such a walk, in the crisp early evening air, and even as it was when she reached the top of the incline she couldn't help being tempted to take a few steps off the path towards the edge of the headland, drawn there by the magnificence of the scenery.

Ilios watched as the wind buffeted Lizzie, whipping her hair into a tangled blonde skein, and then he realised what she was doing.

Lizzie had only gone a few feet when she heard Ilios commanding, from behind her, 'Don't move. Stay where you are.'

It was too much to be denied such a small pleasure on top of everything else, so Lizzie ignored him, determined to defy him and have her moment of small rebellion and triumph even though she had been forced to give in to him on the bigger issues.

When Lizzie ignored him and continued to head for the edge of the promontory, Ilios let go of her case and raced after her.

Too late, Lizzie learned the reason for Ilios's command. The ground was shifting beneath her feet, moving. The edge of the headland was falling away—and she was going to fall with it. She *was* falling, in fact—but not, Lizzie recognised with relief, into the sea with the rock and earth. Instead she fell onto hard, firm ground, clear of the headland, wrapped in Ilios Manos's arms as he grabbed her in a flying tackle, dragging her backwards with a speed and force that sent them both falling to the ground. He had saved her life.

'Are you crazy? What the hell were you trying to do?'

'Not throw myself off the cliff, if that's what you thought,' Lizzie answered. 'Apart from anything else, I haven't got any life insurance. So there wouldn't be any point in trying to kill myself.'

'So you weren't planning some dramatic gesture, claiming you'd rather have death before dishonour?' he taunted her. 'That's just as well, because you'd have been wasting your time since you have already dishonoured yourself with your debt to me.'

'I wasn't trying to do anything other than look at the view.' Lizzie defended herself. 'I didn't know it was dangerous. There aren't any warning signs.'

'There don't need to be any. It's private property, exclusively mine, for my own use and pleasure.'

Lizzie was still in his arms, with the weight of his body pinning her to the ground. She should try to move, she knew, but those words he had used—*private property...exclusively mine...for my own use and pleasure*—had set off a trail of lateral thinking inside her head. Applied to herself, in the context of his insistence on her repayment of the debt she owed him, they were now conjuring up the kind of sensual scenarios that turned her body weak with a reckless longing and filled her with excitement and apprehension.

She wasn't used to feeling like this about any man. She didn't *want* to feel this way about any man—especially not Ilios Manos, who would, she felt sure, take her desire for him and use it against her to punish her. Wanting a man she barely knew wasn't something she had ever imagined would happen to her—her whole way of life, her entire way of thinking, was diametrically opposed to such a possibility. Not for her own protection, but for the protection of her family. To have such feelings now alarmed and terrified her. Lizzie desperately wanted to ignore what she felt, to deny it completely if she could. But it wouldn't let her. It was too strong for her, too determined to make its need felt.

Her heart was thudding under his hand, Ilios recognized, like the beat of the wings of a trapped bird, frantic for its freedom. But, like this land and everything on it, she was his by rights so ancient they were imprinted on every cell of his body. She was his. He was still holding on to her, and against the palm of his hand he could feel the soft, warm swell of her breast, more rounded and fuller than her slenderness had suggested.

Automatically, of its own accord, as though divorced from his thoughts and answerable only to its own need, his palm curved closer to her flesh, the pad of his thumb-tip moving experimentally over a nipple soft at first, but rising immediately to his touch. He cupped her breast fully, stroking her nipple, and his other hand tightened its hold to draw her closer. His body moved so that he could thrust one thigh between the jean-clad flesh of hers.

The world—her world, the world she had thought she knew—had gone crazy, Lizzie acknowledged. The heat burning through her body was surely global warming gone into overdrive. Her breasts—both of them, not just the one he was caressing—were aching to be enjoyed, whilst the knowing male thigh thrusting between her own made her want to lean against it, move against it, open herself to it and to all the delicious sensual possibilities its presence signposted.

This man was…

This man was her enemy!

What was he doing? Ilios had never had any taste for casual, meaningless sex, and yet here he was touching this woman who was lying beneath him as though he was starved for the sensation of her female flesh beneath his hands—as though the desire he could feel pounding through him was so strong, so all-important and demanding, so beyond his own control, that he had no choice other than to submit to it.

As Lizzie pushed him away Ilios released her, infuriated both with himself for his unacceptable and inexplicable need and with her for being the cause of it.

'You had no right to do that,' Lizzie told him fiercely, desperately anxious to establish that *she* was not the one who had started what had happened.

'That wasn't what your body was saying.'

Of course he was bound to have known what she was feeling, a man like him, with that aura he had of sexual power and knowledge. Lizzie's face burned hot with self-conscious awareness of how he had made her feel. She wasn't going to allow him to get the better of her, though. She couldn't afford to.

'You can think what you like,' she told him defensively. 'But I know the truth.'

Of course she did. And the truth was…

She didn't want to think about what the truth was, or what it had felt like to be held in his arms, to be touched by him, to have her senses set alight and her defences laying down their arms in willing surrender. She didn't want to think of anything other than putting as much distance as she could between herself and Ilios Manos as fast as she could.

CHAPTER FOUR

'WHERE are we going?' Lizzie asked uncertainly, once she was back on her feet and Ilios was a safe distance away from her.

'Not to some secluded grotto so I can imprison you like some Greek nymph awaiting the gods' pleasure, where you will be obliged to answer to my every sensual need, if that is what you are imagining. We are merely returning to Villa Manos, which is where I left my car.'

'Villa Manos? That is where you live?' Lizzie queried—after all, it was far safer talking about a villa than it was thinking about the dangerous effect his previous comments had been having on her.

'No. I have an apartment in Thessaloniki, at the top of the Manos Construction office block. The villa is very old, and the building has fallen into disrepair. It was Tino's hope that he could insist that it be bulldozed, because it might present a danger to the holidaymakers visiting the complex he planned to build here—but then I am sure that you already know all about that, since you are partners.'

They had almost reached the top of the incline now, and even though she was slightly out of breath Lizzie turned to face him, her normally calm grey eyes sparkling quicksilver-bright with temper as she objected. 'I have already told you. I have never even met your cousin, never mind been the recipient of his confidences with regard to his business plans.'

'Business plans which included manipulating me into selling him my half of our grandfather's land once he had forced me to remove our ancestral home from it.'

Ilios had started to climb the last few feet of the path, so Lizzie did the same, coming to an abrupt halt as she saw what lay below them, bathed in the last dying rays of the day's light.

At the far end of a long straight drive, lined with tall Cyprus trees and surrounded by Italianate gardens, slightly elevated from the surrounding terrain, set like a pearl against the dark green of the Cyprus and the blue of the Aegean Sea beyond it, perfectly framed by its surroundings was—

'Villa Emo,' Lizzie announced breathlessly in a slightly dazed voice as she stared at the building. She turned to Ilios to say in disbelief, 'It looks exactly like Villa Emo—the house Palladio designed for the Emo family outside Venice.'

To either side of the main house long, low, arcaded wings—which on the original Villa Emo had been farm buildings—extended in perfect symmetry, capped at both ends with classically styled dovecotes, whilst the main building itself was a perfect copy of the Italian original.

'It's so beautiful,' Lizzie whispered, awestruck by the wonderful symmetry of the building and wondering how on earth Palladio's beautiful villa for the Emo family had somehow transported itself here, to this remote Greek Macedonian promontory.

'A deadly beauty, some might say, since it was someone

else's desire to possess it conflicting with my grandfather's determination to keep it that cost my father and Tino's father their lives.' His voice was openly harsh with bitterness.

Without waiting to see if Lizzie was following him he started off down the steep path towards the house. Automatically Lizzie followed him, unable to stop herself from asking, once she had caught up with him, 'What happened—to your father?' She had lost her own parents, after all, and she knew the dreadful pain of that kind of loss.

'What happened?' Ilios stopped so abruptly that Lizzie almost cannoned into him, only stopping herself from doing so by placing her hand on his forearm to steady herself. She snatched it back again for her own safety and peace of mind as she felt the now familiar surge of sensual longing that physical contact with him brought her. How was it possible for this one man to do what no other man had ever done, without actually doing anything to arouse the desire she felt for him? Lizzie didn't know, and she didn't really want to know either. She simply wanted it not to happen.

Ilios was speaking again, and she forced herself to concentrate on what he was saying and not what she was feeling.

'The ruling Junta at the time believed that since my grandfather would not agree to sell the villa to one of their number he should be forced to make a choice between the villa and the lives of his sons. They misjudged my grandfather, I'm afraid. He chose the villa.'

'Over his own flesh and blood?' Lizzie couldn't conceal her horrified disbelief. 'How could he do something like that?'

They had reached the gardens now, and were taking a path that skirted past them, but instead of being disappointed at not being able to see them in more detail Lizzie was too appalled by what Ilios was telling her to think about them.

'He had no other choice,' Ilios told her as they emerged from the shadow of a tree-lined walkway into the gravelled courtyard where he had left his car.

'So what happened—to…to your father?' Lizzie had to ask the question.

'He was shot. They both were. But not at the same time. Tino's father, the younger of the two, was set free initially. It seemed he had convinced the Junta that if they set him free he would persuade his father to change his mind. When he couldn't, the only difference it made to their ultimate fate was that my father was blindfolded and shot by the firing squad he was facing whilst my uncle was shot in the back trying to escape them.'

Lizzie couldn't stop herself from shuddering.

'How awful—your poor mother.'

'I doubt she cared very much one way or the other. She and my father had only been married a matter of months— a dynastic marriage of sorts—and by the time she had given birth to me the Junta had been overthrown.'

Lizzie was appalled.

'So you never knew your father?'

'No.'

'And your mother?'

'She remarried—a cousin with whom she was already in love. I was handed over to my grandfather.'

'She gave you away?'

The pity that had been growing inside her with every terse answer Ilios had given her had grown into an aching ball of shocked compassion. She and her sisters had known such love from their parents, had had such happy childhoods, and Lizzie couldn't help but feel the contrast between her own childhood and the one Ilios must have had.

'As she saw it she had done her duty in marrying my father and producing a son, and so she deserved to follow her own heart, which did not lie with me.'

'Where is she now? Do you see her?'

'She and her second husband were killed in a freak storm when they were out sailing.'

Lizzie could understand why a person would want to keep such a beautiful home in the family—but surely not at the price of one's own children? How could a man have sacrificed his own sons the way Ilios's grandfather had?

'Villa Manos isn't just an inheritance, it is a sacred trust,' Ilios told her coldly, obviously guessing what she was thinking. 'It was said by our ancestor when he had it built that as long as it remained in the hands of the Manos family our family would survive and thrive, but that if it should be lost to the family our line would shrivel and turn to dust. It is the responsibility of the Manos who holds the key to Villa Manos to ensure that there is someone for him to pass it on to. Since he is the elder or the two of us my cousin grew up believing—as I did myself—that our grandfather would pass on the key to him.'

'So why didn't he?' Lizzie couldn't resist asking.

'I went out into the world and made something of myself, whilst Tino preferred to live off what little our grandfather still had. In the end our grandfather decided that our history and out future would be safer in my hands. The land he divided between us, but the house he left to me.'

It was a tale of true Greek tragedy in many ways, Lizzie

reflected as Ilios headed for an expensive-looking car, which Lizzie could now see was a Bentley. He unlocked the passenger door and then opened it for her.

She had no option other than to go with him. Lizzie knew that, but she still hesitated.

In the end it was her compassion for the child he must once have been as much as her awareness of his power over her that had her sliding into the richly luxurious leather seat. Ilios stowed her trolley case in the boot before getting into the driver's seat and starting the car.

What a terrible, tainted inheritance he had received, Lizzie thought sadly as they bumped down the rutted lane.

The March day had darkened into early evening by the time they reached the main road that would take them back to Thessalonica. It had been a long day for Lizzie, who had been up at five in the morning to catch her flight, and the anxiety she had endured added to her tiredness now. Combined with the comforting hum of the expensive car, they had her drifting off to sleep and then waking herself up again as she fought the longing to close her eyes. She might feel appalled by the story he had told her, and filled with compassion for the lonely child he must have been, but that did not mean she felt comfortable about falling asleep in his presence. Far from it. There was something too intimate, too vulnerable about sleeping in his wakeful presence to allow her to do that.

And yet inevitably in the end she was unable to prevent her eyes from closing and her head dropping against the leather headrest, with her face turned towards the man who now had command of her life.

Ilios studied her. The bone structure beneath the pale skin was elegantly formed, her beauty quietly classical and enduring. Her loyalty to her family matched one of the most important tenets of traditional Greek society. She was, he recognised as he looked at her, the kind of woman a man would marry rather than simply want to bed for momentary sexual satisfaction.

Ilios exhaled on the sudden realisation of where his own thought processes were taking him.

The car hit a pothole in the road, waking Lizzie up.

What had she told herself about not betraying any more vulnerability than she had to? she cautioned herself as she sat up, and then frowned as she glanced at her watch and realised what time it was.

'Please excuse me, but I must send a text,' she told Ilios, reaching for her phone.

'To your lover?' Ilios challenged her.

'No! I don't have a lover!' Lizzie denied immediately.

The dark eyebrows rose. 'Such a vehement, almost shocked denial—and yet surely it is perfectly natural that a woman of your age should have a man in her life and her bed. You are what? Twenty-four? Twenty-five? After all, you can hardly still be a virgin.'

'Of course not. And I'm twenty-seven,' Lizzie told him.

Of course not. But her last sexual relationship—her only sexual relationship, in fact—had been when she had been at university. And it had existed more because it was the done thing than because she and the boy in question had envisaged spending the rest of their lives together. Things had been different then. She had been young, and life had been fun. Fun had died out of her life with the loss of her parents.

'And I wasn't shocked. It's simply that I have more important things to think about than men.'

'Such as?'

'My family—my sisters and my nephews. It is actually the boys I need to text. I promised them I would because I won't be there to read their bedtime story—it would have been my turn tonight.' Emotion choked Lizzie's voice. 'My family are far more important to me than any man ever could be. I have to put them first. They depend on me, and I can't let them down. They matter far more to me than some…some fleeting sexual pleasure.'

Automatically Ilios wanted to reject, to push away and in fact deny his awareness of the emotion in Lizzie's voice when she spoke of her family. There was no place for that kind of sentiment in his present life or in his plans for his future life. Nor would there ever be.

'If your only experience of sexual pleasure has been fleeting then it is hardly surprising it doesn't bother you to give it up,' he told Lizzie coolly instead. 'A good lover makes it his business to make his partner's pleasure as enduring as she wishes it to be.'

'That's easy to say,' Lizzie responded, desperate to try to hold her own and appear as nonchalant as Ilios himself. The reality was that his casual observation was having an intense and unwanted effect on her. It was making her ask questions of herself that she knew she could not answer. Questions such as what would it be like to be Ilios Manos's lover?

'And I assure you easy to do, when one knows how,' Ilios came back slipping the comment up under Lizzie's guard and drawing a soft gasp of choked reaction from her.

Of course Ilios Manos would be an experienced lover. Of course he would know exactly how to please his partner—even if that partner was an untutored as she was herself.

She was floundering now, going down under the flood

of awareness surging through her, a flood of dangerous sensations, longings, and—heavens, yes—images as well, of two sensually entwined naked bodies, one belonging to her and the other to Ilios. Stop it, Lizzie warned herself, beginning to panic. She could not afford this kind of self-indulgence. It was far too dangerous.

Determinedly Lizzie concentrated on texting the twins, adding a few words for her sister, telling her that she was still involved in discussions about the letter and would be in touch again as soon as she had something concrete to report to them.

'I take it that your sisters are aware of the purpose of your journey to Greece?' Ilios asked Lizzie.

'Yes,' she agreed. 'They saw your letter.' The thought of how her sisters would feel if they knew what Ilios had said to her—what he had demanded of her—brought a lump to Lizzie's throat. They would be dreadfully shocked—and worried too, for their own security.

That thought had her turning impetuously towards Ilios to beg him emotionally, 'Surely we can come to some kind of sensible arrangement that would enable me to repay you?'

'What do you mean by "sensible"?' Ilios asked.

Lizzie shook her head. 'Perhaps I could work for you as an interior designer?'

'The constructions in which I am involved are very large-scale commercial projects—schools, offices, corporate buildings, that kind of thing. However...' Ilios paused, turning to give her an assessing look in the shadowy darkness of his car. 'There is an alternative means by which you could clear the debt between us.'

Lizzie moistened her suddenly dry lips with the tip of

her tongue, before asking in a voice that was slightly hoarse with tension, 'And that is?'

The Bentley picked up speed as Ilios overtook the car in front of them. The delay in answering her ratcheted up Lizzie's tension.

It seemed an aeon before he turned towards her, his profile outlined by the moonlight beaming into the car. It was an undeniably handsome and very sensually male profile, Lizzie admitted, but there was a harshness in the downward turn of his mouth, that made her shiver inwardly. She wasn't sure which she feared the most: the effect of his harshness on her too easily bruised emotions, or the effect of his sensuality on her equally easily aroused senses.

'Marriage,' Ilios told her.

CHAPTER FIVE

'MARRIAGE?' Lizzie repeated unsteadily, feeling that she must somehow have misunderstood him.

'According to my solicitors I am in need of a wife,' Ilios informed her curtly. 'And since you claim you cannot repay me in cash, and since I have no appetite for the kind of woman who so easily shares her body with any man who has had the price to pay for it, I have decided that this is best way for me to recoup what I have lost and take payment from you.'

Lizzie felt as though glue had been poured into her brain, locking it together and jamming her ability to think.

The only words she could summon were the words, *Ilios Manos*, *marriage*, and *danger*—all written large in bright red ink.

'No,' she told Ilios shakily, before she could do the utterly reckless, dangerous and unthinkable and say yes. Whatever the reason Ilios might want her as a wife, it was absolutely not because he wanted *her*, and she had better hang on to that fact, Lizzie told herself, not start spinning crazily foolish fantasies and daydreams about Mr Right, Cinderella and happy ever after, filled with nights of sensual delight and days of blissful joy.

A categorical no was not the answer Ilios wanted, and nor was it the answer he had expected. He knew of a dozen women at least who would have been delirious with joy at the thought of becoming his wife, quite apart from the fact that Lizzie Wareham was in no position to dare to refuse him anything. She was certainly not going to be allowed to do so. Didn't she realise the position she was in? A position in which he held all the aces and she held none. If not, then perhaps it was time he made that position completely clear to her.

'No?' he challenged her coldly. 'So it is just as I thought. All that you have said to me about your desire to protect your sisters—your family—is nothing more than lies and total fiction.' He paused. A man of action and powerful determination, Ilios did not waste time analysing his decisions once he had made them, or asking himself what might have motivated them—even when they involved the kind of turnaround that had taken place inside his head since that very morning. He had decided Lizzie would be his wife.

He also hated not winning; once he had decided upon a course of action he stuck to it, no matter what obstacles lay in his way. Obstacles could be crushed and then removed. It was simply a matter of finding the right method to do so, with speed and efficiency, and Ilios thought he knew exactly the right method to shift the obstacle to his plans that was Lizzie's 'no'.

'I was about to say—before you were so quick to refuse me—that I am also prepared to pay you a bonus of one hundred thousand pounds, on the understanding that for your part you conduct yourself in public at all times during our enforced relationship as you would were that relationship real. In other words I expect you, in your role as my fiancée and then my wife, to behave.'

A bonus? What he meant was a *bribe*, Lizzie acknowledged, feeling sickened as much by her awareness of how little she could now afford to refuse as by her personal feelings swirling through her at the thought of being married to him.

'To behave as though I'm in love with you?' Lizzie supplied lightly, determined not to let him see how humiliated she felt. The thought of having to act as though she loved him filled her with an immediate and self-defensive need to refuse.

It was bad enough that he was humiliating her by offering her money, without her own painful awareness of her fear that the physical longing he aroused in her so easily might overwhelm her.

A truly brave person did not turn and flee from their own fear and danger, Lizzie reminded herself. A truly brave person stood their ground and fought to overcome it, to make themselves even stronger. And besides, how could she turn down the money he was prepared to offer her when she knew what it would mean at home. It would clear the mortgage, for one thing, and leave nearly ten thousand pounds' much needed 'rainy day money'.

It meant that she would be quite literally selling herself to him—a man she already knew affected her as no man ever had. But she had to accept his offer for the sake of her family. How could she live with herself if she didn't, knowing the huge difference it would make to their lives?

'To behave as though our relationship is genuine and desired by both of us,' Ilios told her. 'Very, well, then.' he continued, when Lizzie remained silent. 'If you prefer to have your family stripped of the roof over their heads—'

What kind of fool was she to dare to try and refuse him? What was she expecting? That he would turn into some

kind of white knight in shining armour? Some kind of
saviour who would generously let her off any kind of
payment? It was time she grew up and learned as he had
had to learn that saviours didn't exist. The only way to
escape from the burdens life presented you with was to dig
your own way out from under them—with your bare
hands, if necessary, as he had. No doubt she expected him
to feel sorry for her, with her tale of how her family had
suffered and how she believed it was her duty to protect
them. Why should he? Who had ever protected *him* when
he had needed protection? No one. Hardship made a
person stronger, unless they were so weak in the first place
that they went to the wall. She must know that herself,
since she had strength.

Ilios frowned. When and how had he decided, without
knowing more about her, that Lizzie Wareham had
strength? Strength was something he admired and re-
spected, after all. Especially when that strength was hard-
won.

'No, of course I don't,' Lizzie told Ilios fiercely, immediately tormented by the horrific images his callous words
had conjured up. 'I just don't understand why you should
want to marry me.'

It was the wrong thing to have said.

'I don't,' Ilios assured her, and the look he gave her
sliced her pride to the bone. 'It is my lawyers who believe
that the best way for me to protect what is rightfully mine
from my cousin's greedy machinations is for me to marry.
Tino needs money. He thinks he can blackmail me into
giving him that money by threatening to challenge my
right of inheritance under our grandfather's will. He knows
that I will never give up what is in effect a sacred charge
on me, a duty to both the history of our name and its future,

so he thinks I will give in to him. But I shall not. He claims that the fact that I am known to have sworn never to marry and do not have a wife means I have broken an unwritten article of faith—namely that Villa Manos must be passed down through the male line of our family. Villa Manos and its lands are a sacred trust. They have been in our family for over five hundred years. They are the essence of what we are. Manos blood, my father's blood, was sacrificed for them. There is nothing I will not do to hold my duty and to meet it. *Nothing!*'

His fury, and the pride that went with it, filled the air around her so that she could almost feel and taste them, Lizzie recognized.

'Tino believes that he has backed me into a corner,' he continued angrily. 'That I will be prepared to buy him off in order to keep Villa Manos. My solicitors advise me that the best and only guaranteed way to block Tino's plans is for me to marry. After all, with blackmail one payment is never the end, it is merely the beginning. If I were to give in to him now—which I have no intention of doing—Tino would think that he has me in his power.'

Privately Lizzie found it impossible to imagine that anyone, male or female, would be foolish enough to think they could control a man like Ilios Manos.

'Why don't you simply find someone you genuinely want to marry?' she suggested. 'After all, a man with your—'

'With my what?' Ilios stopped her. 'With my wealth? That is exactly why I am not married and why I never intend to marry. Only a fool voluntarily puts himself in a position where a woman can enjoy a rich man's money both in marriage and then out of it, after they both discover that they no longer want one another. The curse of wealth is that it has the same attraction for sharks as fresh blood. My marriage to you will be different. You will already have been paid to wear my name and my ring. My cousin does not have the temperament for a long fight. Once he sees that I am married he will lose interest and the marriage can be annulled.'

Lizzie shivered as she heard the implacable merciless coldness in Ilios's voice. It reminded her all too well of what the reality of her situation was.

Once, before their parents' death, she might have been an impulsive eager young woman who believed that one day the sensuality of her nature would find joyous fulfilment with a man who was her soul mate. But that had been a long time ago. Since then she had believed that sensuality and its satisfaction were things she had put to one side without regret. Now, though—albeit against her will—she suspected that Ilios Manos had reignited her female desire. That made her vulnerable to him in a way that could not be countenanced.

For her own sake she should protect herself by returning to England and never thinking about him or seeing him again. For her own sake. But what about her family? For them, for their sake to protect them, she needed to stay here and accept the terms that Ilios was forcing on her. How could she possibly put herself first?

As though he had access to her private thoughts, Ilios told her unkindly, 'You have two choices. Either you agree to marry me, and in doing so give your sisters the financial protection you claim is all-important to you, or you refuse and face the consequences. Because I will pursue you for repayment of your debt to me, with all the power at my command. And I warn you—do not make the mistake of thinking I do not mean what I say or that I will not carry out my retribution.'

Two choices? He was wrong about that, Lizzie admitted bleakly to herself. She had no choice at all.

Even so, she managed to keep her head held high as she told him, 'Very well, then. I shall marry you—although there seems to be something you have overlooked in your calculations,' she couldn't resist adding.

'Which is?' he demanded.

'You said that Villa Manos and its lands must be passed from father to son,' Lizzie pointed out to him.

'And so it shall be,' Ilios agreed. 'We are living in the twenty-first century now,' he told her matter-of-factly. 'A child can be created without its parents having to meet, never mind get married.'

'But what about love?' Lizzie couldn't stop herself from asking. 'You may fall in love, and then—'

'That will never happen. I don't believe in what you call "love", and I don't want to. I would never trust any woman to have my children and not at some stage use them as pawns for her own benefit.'

The harshness in his voice warned Lizzie that this was a dangerous subject, one which raised strong emotions in him, even though she suspected that Ilios himself would refuse to accept that. But not to believe in love—of any kind… Lizzie shivered at the thought of such a cold and barren existence. Love could hurt the human heart—badly—but surely it was also woven into the weft and warp of human life in a way that made it as essential as air and water.

'When the time comes,' Ilios continued, 'I shall ensure that I become the father of one or possibly two sons. They will carry my DNA along with that of a woman who will provide the eggs before being carried by a surrogate. Neither women will know who I am, because it will not be any of their business. My sons will grow up with me, knowing that I am their father.'

'But they will never know their mother.' Lizzie's shock couldn't be hidden. 'Aren't you concerned about how that might affect them?'

'No. Because they will grow up knowing that they were planned and wanted—by me—and why. They will know too that I have protected them from exploitation by any woman using them for her own financial advantage. They will be far too busy learning what it means to be a Manos to worry about the absence from their lives of a woman they can call "Mother". Unlike many other children they will never be in the position of believing that their mother loves them above all else only to find that she does not...'

Was this the reason he refused to believe in love?

'Is that what happened to you?' she asked softly, driven again to feel pity for the child he must have been, despite the way he had behaved towards her. The words were spoken before she could check them.

The softness of Lizzie's voice touched a previously un-recognised area of raw pain within him that immediately had Ilios fighting to deny its existence—furious with himself for having such a vulnerability, and even more furious with Lizzie for so accurately finding it.

'Don't waste your time or your pity trying to psycho-analyse me. All I want from you is payment of your debt to me. Nothing less and nothing more,' he told her coldly.

It was all too much for her to take in, Lizzie admitted numbly. Physical and emotional exhaustion claimed her as the miles flew by, and her eyes ached to be closed just as her mind ached for the panacea of sleep, so that it could escape for a little while from the daunting prospect ahead of her. If it was cowardly to allow herself to find that escape in sleep, then she would just have to be a coward, Lizzie told herself, and she allowed her eyes to close.

He had got what he wanted, so why wasn't he feeling a greater sense of triumph? Ilios wondered. Why wasn't he filled with a sense of righteous satisfaction in having forced Lizzie to make reparation? He had the right and the justification for feeling both of those things, after all.

Some sense he hadn't known he possessed alerted him to the fact that Lizzie had fallen asleep again. He glanced at her. At least she would make a convincing wife—which, of course, was exactly why he had hit on this method of making her pay what she owed him. It was a perfectly logical and sensible decision for him to have made, and one which would leave him with the balance sheet of his pride healthily in credit. That was why he had been able to offer her the additional inducement of a cash payment. There *was* no other reason. No question of him actually having felt some sort of ridiculous compassion for the plight of her family. He simply wasn't that kind of man and never would be. If Lizzie Wareham *was* the victim of circumstance rather than her own greed, as she insisted to him she was, then what was that to him? Nothing.

He had no duty to take the woes of others onto his own shoulders. His duty was solely to himself alone. Because there was only himself. Alone. That was what he was—alone. And that was the way he preferred it, and it always would be.

Ilios put his foot down on the accelerator. His need to focus on the increased speed with which he was driving might be giving him an excuse not to focus on the woman sleeping at his side, but it was not an excuse he needed, he assured himself. Nor was it anything to do with *him* if the angle at which she was sleeping was likely to give her a stiff neck. But his foot was covering the brake in the minute gap between him recognising her discomfort and refuting his need to become involved in it.

Some instinct told Lizzie that something had changed and that she needed to wake up. A scent—alien and pulse-quickening, and yet also familiar and desired—caught at her senses, like the warmth of the heat from another body close to her own, the touch of a hand on her skin. Slowly Lizzie opened her eyes, her heart banging into her chest wall as she realised that she was practically lying flat in the front seat of the Bentley, with Ilios leaning over her. The soft light illuminated the interior of the car, and with it the carved perfection of his features.

Inside her head a tape played, trapping her when she was too vulnerable to stop it, tormenting her with images of herself reaching up to touch his face with her fingertips, exploring its chiselled features. Surely it should be impossible for a real live man to have such classically perfect male features?

She wanted to touch him, to run her fingertips over his face as though he were indeed a marvellous sculpture, created by hands so skilled that one could not help but yearn to touch the masterpiece they had created.

She could almost feel the hard-cut shape of his mouth— the lower lip full and sensual, the groove from the centre of his top lip to his nose clearly marked. A sign of great sensuality, so she had once read. His skin would feel warm and dry, and as she explored the pattern of his lips he would reach out and take hold of her wrist, kissing her fingers.

Frantically Lizzie struggled to sit upright, panicked by Ilios's proximity and the unwanted images inside her head to which it was giving rise.

His sharp, 'Be still', was harshly commanding, his eyes a deep dark gold in the soft light of the interior of the car. Hadn't it been the Greek King Midas whose touch had turned everything before him to gold, thus depriving him of life-giving water and food? Even his son had been turned into a golden statue by his touch, leaving him unable to return his love. Was that what had happened to Ilios? Had the circumstances of his birth and the burden of his inheritance deprived him of the ability to feel love? What if it had? Why should that matter to her?

'There is no cause for you to act like a nervous virgin. I was simply adjusting your seat so that you could sleep in it safety.'

Lizzie's 'Thank you', was self-conscious and stilted.

As he moved back from her to his own seat Ilios told her in a clipped, rejecting voice, 'There's no need to thank me. After all, had you fallen across me my safety would have been compromised as much as yours.'

Lizzie could have kicked herself. Of course he hadn't been thinking about her personal safety. Why should he?

Ilios had noticed her recoil from him—obviously instinctive and unplanned. But he was certainly not affected by it. Far from it. The last thing he wanted was a sexual relationship between them to add complications to the situation. Ilios looked out into the darkness beyond the car. He should perhaps make that clear to her. Not because of his own pride, of course. No. It was simply the sensible thing to do.

Restarting the car, he informed Lizzie dispassionately, 'I should have made it clear earlier that our marriage will merely be a business arrangement. If you were thinking of adding to your bonus payment by offering a sexual inducement, then let me warn you not to do so.'

As Lizzie exhaled in angry humiliation, Ilios continued bluntly, 'I do not want either your body or your desire. Should you be tempted to offer me either one of them, or both, then you must resist that temptation.'

There—that should have made the position clear to her, Ilios decided. It would certainly remove any future risk of his body reacting to her unwanted proximity.

He had obviously realised the effect he was having on her, Lizzie thought miserably.

Annoyingly, now that her seat was reclined and she could have slept comfortably, she felt too self-conscious to do so. So she found the buttons Ilios had used and brought her seat upright again, informing him in as businesslike a voice as she could, 'My sisters will be expecting to hear from me. I think it will be best if I simply tell them I shall be working for you as an interior designer, rather than trying to explain about our…the marriage.'

'I agree. However, where *my* friends and acquaintances are concerned the marriage will obviously become a public reality, and for that reason I think we should agree a suitable history of our relationship. I suggest we say simply that we met when I was on business in England and that our relationship has progressed from there. I kept it and you under wraps, so to speak, until I decided that I wanted to marry you.'

'Until we decided that we wanted to marry one another,' Lizzie corrected him firmly, refusing to give way and break eye contact with him when he flashed her a look of arrogant disbelief that said quite plainly that in his book *he* made the decisions.

'We shall soon be back in the city,' he continued, breaking the challenging silence. 'Which hotel are you in?'

'I had intended to stay in one of the apartments,' Lizzie was forced to admit.

'You mean you haven't booked anywhere?' His tone was critical and irritated, making Lizzie feel foolish and unprofessional. She had so much else on her mind to worry about that she'd completely overlooked the fact that she now didn't have anywhere to stay.

'Like I said, I was expecting to stay in one of the apartments,' she defended herself, telling him, 'Just drop me off somewhere central and I'll find somewhere.'

The last thing she wanted was for him to take her to some five-star hotel she couldn't afford.

Ilios fought back his irritation whilst mentally calculating the risk of how likely it was that someone he knew would see Lizzie and remember her later if he booked her into a hotel. He decided the odds were too high for him to take. It wasn't that he particularly cared about the fact that his wife-to-be wasn't wearing designer clothes, full make-up and expensive jewellery, but local society liked to gossip, and he didn't want anyone asking awkward questions.

They were travelling down a wide thoroughfare, passing a spectacularly well-designed tall glass and marble building, but before she could comment on it Ilios had turned into a side street and driven down a dark ramp, activating a door in the black marble of a side wall that opened to allow him to drive inside.

'Where are we?' Lizzie asked uncertainly.

'The Manos Construction building,' Manos told her. Under the circumstances I think it will be best if you stay in my apartment. There are certain formalities that will need to be dealt with—and quickly, if my cousin's suspicions are not to be alerted. Since you don't already have a hotel booking, it makes sense for you to stay with me.'

Stay with him? Lizzie's mouth had gone dry with tension and anxiety.

'Nothing to say?'

'What am I supposed to say? Thank you?' Lizzie's voice was filled with despair, and her emotions overwhelmed her as she demanded, 'Have you any idea what it's like to be in my position? Not to know whether or not you can pay your bills, or even where your next meal is going to come from? Not having anyone to turn to who can help?'

'Yes. I have known all those things and more—far more than you can ever imagine.'

His answer silenced Lizzie in mid-sentence, leaving her with her mouth half open.

Ilios hadn't intended to allow himself to speak about his most deeply buried memories, but now that he had begun to do so he discovered that it was impossible for him to stop. Emotions—anger, bitterness, resentment—fought with one another to tell their story, bursting from their imprisonment in a torrent of furiously savage words.

'World War Two and everything that followed it destroyed our family fortunes. What it didn't take the Junta did. I left home when I was sixteen, intent on making my fortune as I had promised my grandfather I would. Instead I ended up in Athens, begging from rich tourists. That was how I learned to speak English. From there I got work on construction sites, building hotels. That was how I learned to make money.'

'And you worked your way up until you owned your own business?'

'In a manner of speaking. Only the way I worked myself up was via a spell in prison and a few good hands of cards. I was falsely accused of stealing materials from a site on which I was working. In prison I found that I could make money playing cards. I saved that money, and then I went back to the construction trade and started to put to use what I'd learned.'

He would make a very bad enemy, Lizzie decided, shivering a little as she heard in his voice the implacability that had made him what he was.

What was happening to him? Ilios wondered. Why was he suddenly talking about things he had vowed never to discuss with anyone? It must be because he wanted to ensure that Lizzie Wareham didn't get away with thinking that she was the only one to have had hardship in her life. Satisfied with his answer, Ilios got out of the car and went round to the passenger door to open it for Lizzie.

He looked immaculate, Lizzie noticed, whilst she felt sure that she must look travel-creased and grubby. Whilst she smoothed her jeans, and then tried to do the same to her hair, Ilios went to the boot of the car and removed her case from it. Hastily Lizzie went to take it from him, but he shook his head, carrying it as easily as though it was a sheaf of papers. She had no need to wonder where his muscles came from. All that work on building sites, no doubt.

'The lift's this way,' he told her, directing her towards a marble and glass area several yards away. He activated it with a code he punched into the lock, standing back to allow her to go into the lift first.

If he hadn't told her himself about his childhood she would never have guessed, Lizzie acknowledged. He had the polished manners and self-assurance she associated with someone born into comfortable circumstances, not someone who had come up the hard way. But then his background was obviously moneyed, in the sense that his family had possessed it at one time. Had that made things harder for him? Set him apart from those he'd worked with? Had he ever felt alienated and alone?

Lizzie tried to imagine how she would feel if she didn't have her sisters, and then warned herself that sympathy was the last thing Ilios Manos wanted. He was a man who stood alone because he wanted to stand alone. He had as good as told her that himself.

The lift soared upwards at speed, flattening her stomach to her spine. She'd never really liked lifts, and this one was all glass, on the inside of the cathedral-like space of the building. Even though it was now in darkness, it made her feel distinctly nervous.

The lift stopped swiftly and silently, its doors opening onto an impressive rectangular hallway. The walls and floors were covered in limestone, and concealed lighting illuminated the space, highlighting the pair of matching limestone tables either side of a pair of double doors, cleverly looking almost as though they had been carved out of the wall instead of standing next to it. Two marble busts—one on either table—were also illuminated by concealed lighting.

When he saw her looking at them, Ilios told her, 'They are supposed to have been brought back from Italy by Alexandros Manos at the same time as he returned with copies of Palladio's plans for the villa. If you know Villa Emo and anything of its history then you will know that the Emo family were said to be of Greek descent—hence the classical Greek appearance of the villa.'

'As a trading port, Venice was something of a melting pot for various nations back then,' Lizzie agreed.

Ilios nodded his head, then opened the doors and waited for her to precede him.

A corridor lined with black marble on one side and mirrors on the other, to expand the space, opened out into a large living area with floor-to-ceiling glass walls virtually all along its length. Through them Lizzie could see the night sky, studded with stars.

White sofas stood on a black-tiled floor, focussed on a modern fireplace in the centre of the room. Picking up a remote control, Ilios pressed a button and a wall of the black glass rectangular chimney surrounding the fire slid back, to reveal a large television screen.

Everything in the room was state of the art and a future collector's piece, Lizzie recognised. She could immediately put a name to the prestigious interior design partnership that was responsible for the interior, and even to the designer within that concern who had headed up the team.

'Walt Eickehoven.' Without thinking, she said his name out loud.

Ilios swung round. 'You know him?'

'No, but I know his style,' Lizzie answered. 'Those sofas and that unit are unmistakably his. I've heard that he's got a queuing list of clients that goes into months, if not years.'

Ilios shrugged. 'Queues can be jumped. I'll show you the guest suite, and then you'll need something to eat. I'll order something in—do you like moussaka? If so, we can eat in half an hour.'

Lizzie nodded her head. She was hungry, but she was also tired.

'This way,' Ilios instructed her.

'This way' led down another windowless corridor of marble and mirrors, this one with inset niches, each one containing a carefully lit piece of stone artwork.

The apartment was a work of art in itself, Lizzie recognized, but her heart ached over a private question. How would the two motherless sons Ilios Manos intended to bring up fit into such an environment? She didn't think she would actually want to live in such a polished and sterile atmosphere herself, even though as a designer she could appreciate its stunning design.

Ilios had stopped outside a door in the corridor and was indicating to her. 'I think you will find everything you need inside.'

Nodding again, Lizzie opened the door. By the time she had closed it she knew that Ilios had gone—not because she had seen him go, but because somehow she had sensed it. The air around her and her own body's reaction told her that he was no longer there. She frowned. Finding Ilios Manos sexually attractive was understandable, and she tried to tell herself to quell her growing panic about how she was going to cope living so closely with him. Obviously such a stupendously male man was bound to have that effect on most women. But she was not most women, and she was desperately afraid of her vulnerability. Discovering that he had made such an impact on her senses that even her skin could register his presence or the lack of it was frighteningly dangerous territory—dangerous and not to be risked territory, in fact.

Instead of thinking about the effect Ilios had on her, Lizzie told herself to try and focus instead on her surroundings. As a designer she could possibly learn something that she could take with her into her life, when her present enforced ordeal was finally over.

The guest suite, for instance, was exactly that—a luxurious, streamlined boutique-hotel-style open space, with a sleeping area at one end that contained a bed, and a living space at the other furnished with sofas, tables and a desk.

Like the living room, the guest suite also had a glass wall that ran its full length, but this one looked inward onto what she imagined must be an enclosed garden, since it was virtually on the roof of the building. Carefully placed soft lighting revealed a perspective view of the ruins of a small elevated Greek temple, which looked down into the garden with steps leading from it into a swimming pool. Along the far length of the pool ran a colonnade, planted with vines, which led to a grotto of the sort favoured by designers of the Italian Renaissance opposite the temple. Parterred greenery in intricate formal patterns separated the pool area from the space outside the glass wall, so that that space formed an almost private outdoor sitting area, with double doors from the living space opening out onto it.

Lizzie didn't like to think of the millions just the apartment and its garden must have cost. Professionally, she was in awe. This kind of commission was so far outside her level of operation that the only time she would normally get to view one would be in the pages of a magazine. But, as a woman who shared her own living space with two sisters and twin five-year-old boys, she was almost repelled by the cool, sleek hauteur of living space. It made her feel that as a human being her presence within it spoiled its sterile perfection.

Ilios had handed her trolley case before leaving her, and of course it looked ludicrously out of place.

Half an hour, he'd said. That meant she had the choice of showering and tidying herself up, or texting her sisters.

That choice was no choice, really. Lizzie smiled ruefully to herself as she headed for the double doors to one side of the enormous low-level bed, dressed in immaculate grey and white linen to tone with the slate-grey tiled floor.

Beyond the double doors was a dressing room-cum-wardrobe space—enough space to house the entire wardrobes of her whole family with room to spare—and beyond that, through another set of doors, was the bathroom, containing both a shower and a bath, and a separate lavatory. For the first time since she had entered the apartment Lizzie realised she was in a room that combined both modern artistic design and sybaritic sensuality. For a start, the glass wall continued the full length of the bathroom, making it possible to stand in the wetroom-style shower or lie in the huge stone bath and look out into the garden. Limestone tiles covered floor and walls; thick fluffy grey, white and beige towels were stacked on the inbuilt limestone shelving unit next to the double basins.

After a regretful look at the shower, Lizzie washed her hands and face and then returned to the bedroom, sinking into the white sofa as she quickly texted her family to tell them the good news about her new commission from the owner of Manos Construction.

That done, she only just had enough time to comb her hair and renew her lipstick before a quick glance at her watch told her that her time was up.

When she had made her way back to the living area, she suspected, from the quick frowning glance that Ilios gave her, that he had expected her to have changed clothes. No doubt he was used to women making an all-out effort to impress him, but even if she'd had time to change, Lizzie acknowledged, since all she had to change into was a different top she was hardly likely to have impressed him.

While he might not exhibit the tendencies one somehow expected to see in a man who had 'come from nothing'—for instance, whilst she had no doubt that both his clothes and the watch he was wearing were expensive, they were the opposite of ostentatious—she suspected that designer-clad females were his normal choice of arm candy. Which was perhaps why he considered her sex to be so rapacious.

Their food, delivered whilst she had been in the guest suite, was a simple moussaka-type dish. It was, Lizzie admitted as they sat opposite one another at the polished black glass table, absolutely delicious—as was the wine Ilios had poured to go with it.

It was merely necessity that had prompted him to decide that Lizzie could pay off her debt to him by becoming his wife. He had no personal interest in her whatsoever, Ilios reminded himself as he watched her enjoying her food, plainly not in the least bit concerned about the fact that she was still dressed in workmanlike clothes that did nothing to accentuate her figure and were obviously neither designed nor worn with the idea of arousing male desire. So why did it irk him so irrationally to recognise that she had not made the slightest attempt to attract his attention? Was he really such a stereotypical male? Or was it because, despite the fact that she was not making any attempt to attract him, *he* was very much aware of *her*?

If he was, then it was probably due to the fact that it was some time since he had shared his bed with a woman. He had ended his last relationship after his lover had started trying to pressure him into marriage—over a year ago now, in fact.

If Lizzie's manner irked him then it was surely because, even though his current contact with the female sex was via a variety of social and business-related events, and not on any personal level, he took it for granted that the women he met would be well groomed, dressed in such a way that pleasing the male of the species would be their clear intention.

Ilios looked at her and frowned.

'You will need a new wardrobe before you can appear in public as either my fiancée or my wife,' he informed Lizzie.

'I have plenty of clothes at home. I can ask my sisters to send me some.'

'No.'

'Why not?'

'Why not? Right now you are dressed as though you were a suburban matron whose sole concern is looking after her family. Jeans and a blazer, loafers... A woman who does not seek to attract the attention of a man, and who perhaps would even prefer to repel male attention.' He made a dismissive gesture which stung Lizzie's female pride.

'Not all women are so insecure that they want to advertise their sensuality to the world at large. Some of us prefer to keep that aspect of ourselves private. In fact we take a pride in it,' she told him fiercely.

'Meaning what, exactly?' Ilios demanded. 'Wearing dull clothes and so-called sexy underwear beneath them?'

Lizzie could feel her colour rising and bent her head over her wine glass, hoping that the soft fall of her hair would cloak her blush, as she absentmindedly ran her fingertip round the edge of the glass. The fact was that as her sisters often teased her because she was a silk, satin and lace undies fan, the more feminine the better.

Ilios observed her behaviour, knowing immediately the cause of her flushed face and her reluctance to meet his gaze. What was a matter of far more concern and disbelief to him was the effect knowing that beneath her sensible clothes Lizzie Wareham deliberately chose to wear sensual underwear was having on him physically. It might be over a year since he had last had a lover, but that was no excuse for the images that were filling his mind now, and the reaction they were causing within his own body.

Ilios couldn't remember previously being so glad that he was seated at a table, and was thus able to conceal from a woman's view his body's reaction to her. To have such a painfully hard erection was territory that belonged to young men not yet able to fully master their sexuality—not men in their mid-thirties, and certainly not him. The mind could play tricks on a person, he reminded himself, and his reaction was probably not to Lizzie Wareham but to images he himself had created. He did not desire her. He was, to put it bluntly, simply aroused. He could have put any attractive female body into those images and felt the same effect. Desiring Lizzie Wareham was not part of his plan, and therefore must not be allowed to happen.

'I have work to do, so I suggest that you take the opportunity to go to bed have an early night,' he informed Lizzie.

He didn't want her out of the way because her presence was disturbing him on an intensely personal and sensual level that he didn't like. Not for one minute.

Lizzie's head lifted, her face burning even more hotly as her body immediately responded to the word *bed*—and not in a way that had anything to do with going to sleep. Somehow her senses refused to accept that anything as mundane as sleeping could take place in a bed that was in any way connected to Ilios Manos. Which was, of course, totally ridiculous. She was reacting like some hormone-flooded pubescent teenager, quivering with embarrassingly super-strength lust.

'Yes, I am tired,' she managed to respond. She was doing the mental equivalent of running past something dangerous without risking looking at it, determinedly avoiding re-using the word 'bed', Lizzie derided herself. But what else could she do, with her body signalling with increasing intensity the excited pleasure with which it viewed the prospect of going to bed with Ilios Manos? Not that *that* was going to happen. He had told her so already. Theirs was purely a business arrangement, that was all, and that was the way it was going to stay. Somehow she would find the strength to make sure that it did.

CHAPTER SIX

'I HAVE a meeting in half an hour.' Ilios stood up to finish the cup of coffee he was drinking whilst Lizzie remained seated, seeing him glance at his watch before continuing.

'I've ordered suitable clothes for you via an online concierge service. They should arrive within the hour. Have a look through them. If there's anything that doesn't fit, let me know. There's no need to thank me.'

'I wasn't going to,' Lizzie assured him grimly.

Ignoring her comment, Ilios continued, 'We shall be attending a gallery opening this evening, so you'll need to wear an engagement ring. I'm having a selection couriered over to my office. Maria should arrive at some stage to do the cleaning.' He reached into the inside pocket of his suit jacket and removed his wallet, opening it and removing what looked to Lizzie like an obscene amount of one-hundred-euro notes.

'You'll need this, I dare say. And I've put my mobile number into your mobile's address book. I should have thought that in view of the fact that you're an interior designer you would have had a more stylish one. Appearances count, after all.'

'I agree, but paying for luxury gizmos costs money,'

Lizzie defended, Her out-of-fashion mobile was nonetheless perfectly effective.

Five minutes later, left to her own devices in a space in which the smell of rich coffee and maleness lingered dangerously to torment her senses, Lizzie decided to explore her new surroundings—starting with the garden.

She could see now in daylight that the living space did not overlook the city, as she had expected, but instead had views towards the mountains.

The intercom buzzing had her heading for the entrance of the apartment, mindful of what Ilios had told her. When she opened the door there was no sign of a delivery person, but there were several large boxes stacked next to the door.

Nearly two hours later, standing in the guest bedroom surrounded by the clothes she had unpacked, Lizzie wished more than anything else that her sisters were here with her, to stare in awe at the beautiful garments now covering the bed.

The clothes *were* beautiful, and in exactly the kind of style she had always secretly coveted.

Out of the corner of her eye Lizzie caught sight of the deliciously pretty and feminine underwear she had hastily pushed out of sight under some of the day clothes, her face warming. Obviously he had noticed her reaction to his observation the night before. Stunningly sensual undies in soft cream silk and satin, trimmed with lace—or rather laces, she amended ruefully, remembering the boned corset that laced up at the back which had been in one of the boxes. That was something that would quite definitely be going back! After all, she had no one to fasten her into it, even if she had wanted to wear something so constricting. Neither was she entirely sure about the French knickers that were little more than a satin gusset-cum-G-string attached to fluted sheer lace panels. On the other hand the pure silk-satin low-rise boxer shorts and matching bras were so delicious they had made her mouth water.

And as for everything else—how was she supposed to resist the allure of silk cashmere cut into the most flattering skirt and trousers she had ever seen, in her favourite shade of warm beige? The trench coat, in a sort of off-white—not grey, and not beige either—carrying a very famous label, was the exactly the kind of coat she had secretly lusted after ever since she had realised what good clothes were, and it fitted her perfectly.

There were sweaters and shirts, tops, beach clothes, evening clothes, new jeans by an über-fashionable designer, and shoes so plain and yet so beautiful that Lizzie had simply wanted to hug them tightly to her. These were clothes that spoke an international language—and that language was the language of discreet style and elegance and an awful lot of money.

Lizzie stroked the silk tweed of a three-quarter-length Chanel coat in black and white, with the trademark Chanel camelia attached to an equally trademark Chanel chain fastening. How could she accept all of this? She couldn't. It was too much. She needed clothes, yes—but far less than this.

With a small sigh she began to repack what she thought were the more expensive items, retaining only what she felt she would genuinely need. Packing away the silk cashmere skirt and trousers and the Chanel coat and skirt and blouse wasn't easy, but it had to be done, Lizzie told herself firmly.

She had just finished, and was about to carry the boxes to the front door, when she heard a firm knock on the bedroom door.

Maria, the cleaner, must have arrived, Lizzie guessed—but when she went to open the door it was Ilios, who was standing in the corridor, looking impatient.

'I'm sending these back,' Lizzie told him, indicating the boxes she had just packed.

Ilios surveyed them, noting that there were far more by the door than there were on the floor beside the bed.

'They didn't fit? You didn't like the style?' His voice sharpened slightly. He still didn't know why he had changed his mind at the last minute and told the concierge service to select clothes for a woman who preferred discreet stylishness to clothes that were sexy.

This wasn't the kind of man who liked being proved wrong—about anything, Lizzie acknowledged, even when it was the dress size of a woman he had only just met. Because he felt that he was being judged and found wanting? Because it was important to him to prove himself as a success in every aspect of his life? Because inside there was still a part of him that had grown up knowing that his father had been sacrificed for a building, with all the fear for his own safety and security that must have caused? Stop feeling sympathetic towards him, she warned herself. It will only make things worse.

'No, they were perfect—both in fit and style,' she assured him.

'So why are you sending them back?'

'I don't need them, and… Well, they were far too expensive. The kind of clothes I could never afford. I would have preferred it if the clothes had been less expensive.'

It took Ilios several seconds to adjust his own thinking and judgement to her words. A woman who genuinely did not want a man to spend money on her? Who did she think she was kidding? Ilios didn't believe that such a woman existed.

'You will not be living the kind of life you normally live. As my fiancée and then my wife I expect you to dress and behave as the kind of woman those who know me would expect me to marry. You must think of yourself as an actress and these clothes as your props. You will not feel confident amongst my friends if you are not dressed appropriately.'

'Clothes are only window dressing. True confidence comes from a person's belief in themselves as someone of value,' Lizzie felt bound to point out gently.

'I agree,' Ilios told her unexpectedly. 'But we live in a society in which we are judged by those who do not know us on our outward appearance. For my wife to be seen in chainstore clothes could cause the kind of gossip that might well ultimately lead to speculation in the press that Manos Cosntruction is in financial difficulty. It isn't just my own wealth that depends on the continued success of my business. It is the jobs of all those who work for me. In business, a good reputation can be ninety per cent of one's success—lose that and you stand to lose everything. You must know that.'

There was enough truth in what he was saying for Lizzie to nod her head.

'I have brought a selection of rings in different styles and sizes for you to look at. Whichever one you choose can be sized properly for you.'

Recognising that Ilios was waiting for her to precede him out of the room, Lizzie edged her way past the end of the bed, so desperate to avoid accidentally coming into physical contact with him that she bumped into the bed itself and half stumbled, provoking exactly what she had feared. Ilios reached out to steady her, his hand resting firmly against her waist. His attention, though, was focussed on the floor. Following his gaze, Lizzie's heart sank. There, lying on the floor at his feet, was the corset she had been looking at earlier, which she must have dislodged as she stumbled. Still holding her waist, Ilios bent down and picked it up. He looked at it.

'It's going back,' Lizzie told him immediately. 'I couldn't possibly wear it.'

Ilios looked at her. 'Why not?'

'Well, for one thing it's not the type of thing I would wear, and for another I'd need someone to fasten it for me—it laces up at the back,' she explained. 'And that means that I'd need...'

'A man?' Ilios supplied for her.

'Another pair of hands,' Lizzie corrected him. The warmth of his hand on her waist was causing havoc inside her body. An entire quiverful of tiny, fiery darts of sensual pleasure seemed to have been discharged into her body, unleashing a thousand pinpoints of sensory reaction—rivulets of female need that were speedily flowing into one another to form a dangerously fast-flowing flood of physical desire.

Inside her head that desire was painting dangerous images. As though by magic what she was wearing had been removed and she was reclothed in the satin underwear she had been admiring before Ilios had arrived. At the same time, equally magically, Ilios's hand was stroking from her hip up to her breast, whilst his lips caressed the equally eager curve where her shoulder met her neck and his free hand slid into the silk-satin to cup the rounded flesh of her bottom.

Frantically Lizzie wrenched her attention away from what was going on inside her head. Ilios was a very attractive man, and it had been a very long time since she had...

Well, it had been a very long time. But that did not give her imagination carte blanche to indulge itself with those kind of totally impossible scenarios—especially in view of what he had said to her about what he did and didn't want from their relationship.

Lizzie pulled herself free of Ilios's hold and headed for the door, leaving Ilios to look thoughtfully at the corset and then at her disappearing back view, before dropping the corset onto the bed and turning to follow her.

'These are the rings. I asked the jeweller to send a variety for you to choose from.'

Lizzie's eyes widened as she looked down at the rings in the large leather case that Ilios had opened.

There were solitaires in a variety of shapes and cuts, coloured diamonds surrounded by diamonds, diamonds surrounded by diamonds—so much, in fact, that the light reflected from the rings almost dazzled her.

'They're all beautiful,' she told Ilios. 'But they're so...so eye-catching and big. Couldn't I have something smaller?'

'How much smaller?' Ilios asked dryly.

Lizzie pointed to one of the rings and told him, 'About a quarter of the size of that one. And plain. Just a solitaire.'

'Something more like this, do you mean?' he asked, reaching into his pocket and removing a small box which he opened to reveal a plain, perfectly plain solitaire set in what Lizzie assumed must be platinum, on a narrow platinum band.

Ilios didn't really know why he had noticed the ring, nor what it was about it that had made him think of Lizzie, never mind why he had asked for it to be boxed separately, but he could see from Lizzie's expression how she felt about it.

The ring was so simple and so perfect that Lizzie fell in love with it immediately.

'Exactly like that,' she told him.

Ilios removed the ring from the box and held it out to her, and for some reason—automatically, really, without thinking about what she was doing—rather than take it from him Lizzie extended her finger towards him instead.

Ilios looked at her, and she looked back at him, and a quiver of something age-old and beyond logic shot through her. Neither of them spoke. Instead Ilios curled his fingers round her wrist and then slowly slid the ring onto her wedding ring finger.

It fitted her perfectly. It looked and felt as though it had been made for her—as though it had been meant for her.

'It's perfect.'

Emotion choked her voice and stung her eyes. The ring was an age-old symbol of human love and commitment, given to bind a couple together, and suddenly it seemed to possess a significance that touched her far more deeply than she had expected.

'I wasn't expecting you back until later. You said you had a lunch engagement.' How strained and vulnerable she sounded—like someone desperately trying to make polite conversation as a means of covering up the huge, yawning dangerous pit that had suddenly opened up in front of them.

'The lunch was cancelled.' He was not going to tell her that he was the one who had done the cancelling.

'This gallery-opening you said we'd be attending this evening, will it—?' Lizzie began

'It will be a high-profile media event—lots of society

faces and photographers,' Ilios interrupted. 'Lots of gossip and champagne—you know the kind of thing. I have to go. I've got a site meeting in half an hour.'

Lizzie just nodded her head.

CHAPTER SEVEN

SHE wasn't doing this for Ilios, she was doing it for herself—to prove to herself that she had the strength to deal with this latest obstacle in her life the same way in which she had dealt with all the others: that was with courage and fortitude and a determination that those who needed her and depended on her would not find her wanting, Lizzie told herself firmly as she studied her reflection in the guest suite's dressing room mirror.

Matt black jersey draped her body from her throat to her knees, the dress's long sleeves ending on her wrists. A discreet sparkle of tiny jet beads in the shape of a flower just below her left shoulder was the dress's only ornamentation, but the way the fluid Armani dress moved when she moved really said everything about it that needed to be said, Lizzie knew.

Having had the whole afternoon in which to get ready, and having slipped out to buy a selection of glossy fashion magazines so that she could study the social pages, Lizzie could now understand why Ilios had deemed it necessary to replace her existing clothes. Greek women she could see did not believe in cutting corners or making economies about when it came to making a style statement. Designer labels, expensive jewellery, impeccable make-up and enviably glossy hair were, it seemed, *de rigueur*, and it was something she had decided she could not match without professional help.

As a result, and with Ilios's warning very much to the forefront of her mind, she had gone back out in search of a hairdresser. Now, thanks to Ilios's euros and the welcome skill of a Greek hairdresser, her hair was framing her face in a soft 'up do' that managed to be both elegant and yet at the same time look softly feminine, with delicate loose tendrils of hair drifting round her temples and down onto her neck, and her nails were immaculately manicured. Lizzie had refused the dark red polish the manicurist had offered—somehow it hadn't seemed appropriate for a newly engaged woman: far too aggressive and challenging. However, conceding that anyone genuinely newly engaged to Ilios would want the world to know about it by showing off her ring, she had agreed to a muted pink polish, because it matched her favourite lipstick shade.

She looked at her watch. It was not the pretty Cartier her parents had given her when she had obtained her degree—she had passed that on to Ruby when the twins had been born—but a plain, serviceable chainstore watch. Half past six. Ilios should be back soon, and she didn't want him to have to come knocking on the bedroom door a second time to find her.

Picking up the black clutch bag that went with her high-heeled suede shoes, and the pure white cashmere coat that was surely the most impractical garment even created, Lizzie opened the door and stepped out into the corridor, giving Ilios, who was standing at the other end of it on his way to his own room, the perfect opportunity to study and assess her appearance.

'Well?' she challenged him. 'Do I look suitably high-maintenance and worthy of being your fiancée?'

To say that he was lost for words would be an exaggeration, Ilios decided, but to admit in the privacy of his own thoughts that the Lizzie standing at the other end of the corridor waiting for his response was a woman whose discreetly sensual elegant took his breath away would not.

When Lizzie saw Ilios frown her heart sank, even whilst her pride stiffened. If she wasn't good enough for him, then too bad. After all, *she* wasn't the one who had insisted upon their fake relationship.

'You'll need these,' Ilios announced harshly, holding out to her several boxes without answering her question, and then walking away from her in the direction of the master bedroom.

Unwillingly, Lizzie took the boxes from him. Don't you dare cry, she warned herself as she went into the living area. She didn't dare, with the amount of mascara she had on.

Would it really have been so difficult for him to tell her that she looked good, even if he didn't really think so? He must know how anxious she was feeling. How much she needed the confidence his support would have given her.

Dropping her coat onto one of the sofas, Lizzie opened the first of the boxes, her eyes widening in disbelief as she looked at the contents. The necklace sparkling on the velvet couldn't possibly be real, could it? All those diamonds—and a matching bangle. She closed the box quickly. Her dress might look vaguely *Breakfast at Tiffany's*, but she certainly wasn't going to risk wearing something that might be worth a king's ransom just to reinforce that image.

She was about to open the other boxes when Ilios returned.

He'd obviously showered, because his hair was still damp—and not just on his head. Lizzie had to fight to drag her gaze away from the damp, dark silky body hair she could just see as he finished fastening his shirt. His unexpected request for help as he opened his palm to reveal a pair of cufflinks startled her as she refocussed her gaze. Her mouth instantly went dry as a slow ache uncurled inside her body—like woodsmoke, and just as dangerously pervasive.

Somehow she managed to scramble to her feet and go to him, taking the links from him. Rose-gold and plain, they felt soft and warm in her palm. The initials on them were slightly faded, although she could still make out the interlaced A and M. Almost absently she rubbed her fingertip over them.

'They were my father's.' She heard Ilios's voice somewhere above her head. 'The design is Venetian. It is a tradition in our family that when a boy reaches the age of maturity he is given a pair of such cufflinks by his father—a sign of his manhood. Since my father was not able to do that for me, I wear his instead.'

For the second time in less than half an hour Lizzie had to remind herself of the damage tears would do to her eye make-up.

Watching Lizzie's head, bent towards his wrist, the nape of her neck exposed to his gaze, Ilios had to resist the temptation to reach out and curl one of the small escaping fronds of hair round his finger. He could quite easily have fastened the cufflinks himself—far more easily than Lizzie, in fact—but for some reason he had decided to ask her to do it for him. As a test of her suitability to be his wife? he taunted himself. Or as a test to himself, to prove he was not as susceptible to her as his body insisted on repeatedly telling him he was?

She really wished she wasn't having to do this, Lizzie admitted. Her fingers were stiff with nervousness and yet at the same time they were trembling. She could smell the scent of Ilios's freshly showered body, mixed with some kind of discreet male cologne, and whilst she wouldn't have said that the effect it was having on her senses was making her want to rip open his shirt and bury her face against his torso, it wasn't far short of that.

It was a relief to finally complete her task and be able to step from him, draw in a gulp of hopefully steadying and non-Ilios-smelling air.

'You aren't wearing your jewellery.'

'I…I thought it might be a bit too much.'

The dark eyebrows rose. 'I disagree. You should wear it.'

Because if she didn't she'd look out of place. That was the unspoken message he was giving her, Lizzie recognised as she picked up the two smaller boxes and opened them. She had to blink at the magnificence of the diamond earstuds in front of her. They had to be at least a carat each, and so brilliant they dazzled her.

Quickly Lizzie slipped them into her ears. With her hair up she did need something, she acknowledged. But merely 'something'—not these dazzling and no doubt very expensive earrings.

'What's wrong?' Ilios demanded.

'I was just thinking how many families the price of these would feed. It seems wrong to wear something like this when so many people are going through such a hard time. It makes me feel uncomfortable.'

'So if I were to offer them as a gift you would rather I gave their value in money to a charity? Is that what you're saying?' Ilios taunted her.

'Yes,' Lizzie responded—truthfully and without hesitation.

'Put on the watch, and then we had better leave,' was all Ilios said in response.

She was lying, of course; she had to be. He wasn't deceived or taken in by her, nor would he ever be—by her or by any other woman.

The watch was discreetly expensive: a plain black leather band and a white-gold face was studded with small diamonds.

Since Ilios was already shrugging on his suit jacket, Lizzie fastened the watch quickly and went to pick up her coat—just as Ilios too was reaching for it. Their fingertips met and touched, his over her own, warm and strong, filling Lizzie with a need to simply curl her fingers into his in a silent plea for acceptance and comfort.

Frantically she pulled back, grabbing hold of her coat with her other hand and telling Ilios quickly, 'It's all right. I don't need to put it on. I'll just carry it until we get out of the car.'

She really didn't think she was up to any more physical contact right now, with a man whose mere presence seemed to have the ability to send her body's awareness of him to stratospheric levels.

The gallery, when they reached it, was ablaze with lights, and with the shine reflected from the stunning amount of diamond jewellery being worn. Ilios's hand was on Lizzie's arm as he guided her through the mass of paparazzi, waiting to snap photographs of the rich and famous as they made their way from the kerb to the door.

'I can see now why you aren't keen on my outfit. Obviously to be considered anything like worthy of you I'd have to have dressed very differently,' Lizzie was forced to admit reluctantly once they had stepped inside. She had seen how many of the other women were wearing tiny little dresses, bandaged—or so it seemed—to their equally tiny bodies. The dresses revealed lengths of lean bronzed leg and the swell of quite often implausibly taut and rounded breasts.

No wonder he had derided her choice of clothes if this was what he considered normal clothing for the female body.

'The women you are looking at are high-price tarts up for sale—on the hunt for the richest husband they can snare,' Ilios told Lizzie grimly. 'The clothes they are wearing denote their profession, as does their desire to be photographed. It's their version of newspaper advertising. Come with me.'

As though by magic the mass of bronzed flesh parted to let them through—although not without some very predatory and inviting looks being thrown in Ilios's direction, Lizzie noticed.

Beyond the call girls and the men hanging round them, in the interior of the gallery were several groups of people: men in business suits, and elegant, confident-looking women in beautiful designer clothes.

One of the men came forward, extending his hand.

'Ilios, my friend. It is good to see you.'

'You only say that, Stefanos, because you hope to persuade me to buy something,' Ilios responded, turning to Lizzie to say easily, '*Agapi mou*, allow me to introduce Stefanos to you. I should warn you, though, that he will insist on presenting us with some hideous piece of supposed art as a wedding gift.'

Agapi mou—didn't that mean *my love*? But of course she wasn't, Lizzie reminded herself, as she admired the clever way in which Ilios had announced both their relationship and their impending marriage.

Within seconds people were crowding round them, smiling and exclaiming, and Lizzie had no need to fake the sudden shyness that had her moving instinctively closer to Ilios, so that he took hold of her hand and tucked it though his arm.

'Ilios, how can this be? You have always sworn never to get married.'

The speaker was a woman of around Ilios's own age; she was smiling, but there was a certain hard edge to her voice that warned Lizzie she was someone who might have a shared history with Ilios. She might not entirely welcome the news of his supposed intended marriage, even though she was wearing a wedding ring and was accompanied by a solid, square-faced man who appeared to be her husband.

'Lizzie changed my mind, Eleni,' Ilios answered her, and the smile he gave Lizzie as he turned to look down at her made her suspect that if he had gifted her with that kind of smile and meant it she'd have been transfixed to the spot with delight.

'Well, you cannot cling together all evening like a pair of turtledoves.' Eleni replied. 'I want you to convince Michael that he should build me a new villa on the island—and you, of course, must construct it. There is no other builder to whom we would entrust such a commission. I have it in mind to copy your own Villa Manos for us, since you insist on refusing to let us buy the original from you.'

Immediately Lizzie felt Ilios stiffen, his arm rigid against hers.

So, if they had once been lovers the parting had not been an amicable one, Lizzie guessed. Because there was plainly ill feeling between them now. Eleni must surely know that Ilios would never sell his family home.

'Has Ilios shown you Villa Manos yet, Lizzie? Told you that he will expect you to make your home there once you are married? Personally, I could never live anywhere so remote. Certainly not all year round. And then, of course, one must wonder what one's husband is getting up to whilst he is here in Thessaloniki and you are stuck on a peninsula in the middle of nowhere.'

'I would never marry a man I couldn't trust implicitly,' Lizzie responded calmly, and with quiet dignity.

'My dear, how very brave of you.' Eleni was positively purring. 'I hate to tell you this, but whilst a man will promise anything whilst he is in the first throes of…love, marriage often brings about a sea change. When a woman is occupied with her home and her children her husband can start to look elsewhere for entertainment. Especially a Greek man. After all, they have the example of our Greek gods before them. Zeus himself could not be faithful to his wife. He had many adventures outside their marriage, if mythology is to be believed.'

'A man who is truly happy in his marriage does not seek satisfaction outside it, Eleni, and I know that with Lizzie I shall find all the happiness I need.' Ilios defended their relationship, turning to her to lift her hand to his lips and tenderly kiss her fingers whilst gazing into her eyes.

Ilios really should have been an actor, Lizzie decided, struggling against the tide of longing surging through her. She had to be strong, she reminded herself. She had to fight the effect he had on her. She had to prove to herself that she could endure and overcome the effect his closeness had on her.

'An ex, I take it?' she couldn't resist murmuring to Ilios once they had escaped.

'Of a sort,' he agreed, a little to her surprise. 'Although the prey she was hunting was my cousin, not me. When she discovered that he wasn't going to inherit Villa Manos she dropped him.'

'And turned her attentions to you?'

'She tried,' Ilios agreed. 'But without success. You handled Eleni extremely well,' he said, then paused. Unable to stop himself, he told her brusquely, 'You play your part well. I suspect that every man here is envying me.'

What on earth had made him say that, even if it was true? Why should he care if other men wanted her? The admiration he could see in their eyes was a benefit to him, because it meant that she was being accepted and acceptable as his wife-to-be.

Lizzie couldn't help smiling at him. There was a soft, warm feeling inside her body—a sweet, tender unfolding of something, happiness, that lifted her. Just because Ilios had—what?—complimented her? She must not feel like that. She must not.

What he had said to her was the truth, Ilios knew. But more than that she had a warmth that drew people to her. He had seen it in the eyes of his friends and in their manner towards her. Could he have been unfair to her, wrong about her and the way he had initially judged her? What if he had? He didn't owe her anything, after all. She was the one who was indebted to him, not the other way around.

Lizzie wasn't sorry when it was time to leave the restaurant where they had had dinner with Ilios's friends, next door to the gallery. Whilst the other people she had met had more than made up for Eleni's bitchiness with their warmth and readiness to befriend her, and the food at the smart restaurant had been delicious, she had felt on edge—knowing that she was only playing a part, afraid of making a slip that would reveal the truth, and at the same time uncomfortable with the deceit she was having to practise.

A valet brought the car round, and within minutes of leaving, or so it seemed, they were back in the apartment.

'I've set everything in motion for our wedding,' Ilios told her. 'It will be a civil ceremony, conducted at the town hall. Normally couples having civil ceremonies go on to celebrate more traditionally with a family party, but in our case that won't be necessary. I have let it be known that it is because I am so impatient to make you my wife that we are dispensing with a more lavish affair.'

Lizzie nodded her head, relieved that she had her back to him and he wouldn't see the effect his words were having on her. Tonight, posing as his wife, sometimes almost forgetting that she was simply playing a part, she had felt filled with happiness and…

And what?

And nothing, Lizzie assured herself hastily as she removed the watch and then took out the diamond earrings. Her hands were trembling slightly as she remembered how she had felt tonight, standing at Ilios's side, wanting him, wishing that he would turn to her and look at her with that same longing and need she felt for him.

What she felt for him was quite simply lust. Very shocking, of course, but even so far safer than becoming emotionally drawn to a man who didn't want her.

One of the diamond earrings slipped from her fingers. Just in time Ilios put his palm beneath her own and caught it. Caught it, as somehow he had caught her in the net. If he knew he would throw her to one side, like a fisherman throwing back an unwanted catch. Lizzie looked up at him—and then wished she had not.

Not trusting herself to take the earring from him—because that meant touching him—Lizzie held out the jewellery box to him instead.

Exactly what point was she trying to make by refusing to take the earring from him? Ilios questioned as he dropped it into the box. That she was sexually indifferent to him? If so, why should it make him want to take hold of her and kiss her until her mouth softened beneath his and she was pleading with him for more than mere kisses?

Silently Lizzie collected the scattered jewellery boxes and offered them to Ilios.

'Keep them yourself. You will need to wear them again,' he told her curtly.

Lizzie shook her head. 'I'd rather not. As I said before, they are far too valuable, and they should be in a safe.'

It was gone midnight. There was no reason for her to remain here in the living room with him—not when being with him was so very dangerous for her, she reminded herself sternly, just in case she was tempted to linger. Her will-power seemed to have become far too fragile. She had spent the evening pretending that they were intimately close, as lovers, aided in doing so by the two and a half glasses of champagne she had drunk at the gallery. All those bubbles were bound to have an effect on anyone's system, never mind someone who was quickly discovering how vulnerable she was to the man in front of her.

Her brief, 'I'll say goodnight', merely elicited a brief nod of his head from Ilios. His back was already turned towards her as she opened the door into the corridor.

Maria had obviously been in, Lizzie noted, because the bed was made up immaculately, as though for a new guest.

She went into the dressing room and opened one of the wardrobe doors, intending to undress and hang up her clothes, only the wardrobe was empty. Quickly Lizzie checked the others, and then the drawers. They were empty too. And her case had gone. Along with her toiletries and her toothbrush.

She began to panic. What was going on? She'd have to tell Ilios.

She found him in the living room, standing in front of the glass wall in his suit trousers and his shirt, a glass of wine in his hand. When he turned round as she approached him the shirt pulled across the muscles in his back, causing an aching sensation to slide through her lower body.

'I can't find any of my things,' she told him helplessly. 'They've all disappeared—everything, including my case and even my toothbrush. The maid's been in, because the bed is made up.'

'I know.'

'You know?' Lizzie looked at him uncertainly. What was going on? Had he decided he didn't like her new clothes after all and sent them back?

'They're in my room.'

'What?'

Ilios shrugged irritably. It had been as much of an unwanted discovery for him to find Lizzie's things in the master bedroom as it had obviously been for her to discover that they were missing from the guest room. The main source of Ilios's irritation, though, was his own slip-up in not realising that this might happen.

'Maria obviously took it upon herself to move them. She'll have heard that we are to marry, and it seems she has decided that since we are probably already sharing a bed, she might as well make life easier for herself by moving our things into my room.'

'But we aren't. I mean we can't.' Lizzie was aghast. 'Everything will have to be moved back. I'll do it myself—tomorrow—when you aren't here—but you'll have to tell her.'

'I don't think that would be a good idea.'

'Why not?'

'Because the last thing we want is for her to start gossiping that we're sleeping in separate beds.'

'But you said our marriage would be…that it wouldn't be…that we wouldn't be sharing a bed.'

'I hadn't thought things through properly then,' Ilios was forced to admit.

He was actually admitting that he had got something wrong? Lizzie could scarcely believe it.

'If you're concerned about what Maria might say, then why don't you tell her not to come? I can do her work whilst I'm here,' she suggested helpfully.

Ilios was already shaking his head.

'And deprive Maria of her the money she earns? No. Maria's family are dependent on her wages, and Maria enjoys a certain status in her community because she works for me. It wouldn't be right or fair to deprive her of those things.'

Lizzie had to gulp back the chagrin she felt at being reproved by Ilios for her lack of awareness of the needs of others—chagrin that was all the more intense because previously *she* had seen the one to point out that lack of awareness to him.

'But I don't want to share a…a bed,' she protested. How ridiculous that she had to struggle to force herself to say the word *bed*. She, an interior designer, who in the course of her work was perfectly familiar with those three small letters. Familiar with the letters, but not familiar at all with the way the word *bed* made her feel when she was in the presence of Ilios Manos.

'Do you think I do?' Ilios challenged her, immediately making her feel humiliated. 'We don't have any choice. Fortunately it is a very large bed,' he told her grimly.

She should, of course, be delighted and relieved that her presence in his bed was so unwelcome, Lizzie told herself. She wanted and needed him not to want her—if only to protect her from her own feelings after all. But instead she was filled with an explosive mix of emotions and sensations—heady excitement, tingling suspense, an irrational and rebellious aching longing that defied all her attempts to subdue it, and that was only the start of it. She could have written a list a metre long of all the effects Ilios was having on her as a woman.

She wasn't immature or unread; she knew that it was perfectly possible for a human being to experience sexual desire without necessarily being in love with the person they desired. However, she had never somehow expected to be one of those human beings who *did* feel like that. She had assumed that only those women with a high sex drive were likely to have their hormones drooling with longing for a man to whom they had no intention of becoming emotionally attached. But now, of course, she knew better. Much, much better. And what she knew told her very definitely that she could not risk sharing a bed with Ilios. Not under any circumstances. Of course she could and would attempt to control her feelings, but what if she failed? What if she was tempted to—? But, no—she must not, under any circumstances, allow those tormenting images she had viewed before to slip into her head.

It was a large bed, Ilios had said. But far from tamping down the fire running riot inside her, his words had only fed it. A large bed meant more space in which to enjoy the sensuality of all the delights the human body could provide.

Lizzie could feel the prickle of the nervous sweat breaking out on her skin. This couldn't go on. If it did she might well end up doing something she would not only regret but which would cause her humiliation and shame. She felt sick with anxiety. She could not share a bed with him. She simply didn't trust herself to be able to do so without giving in to temptation. Even if by some miracle she could control herself whilst she was awake, who knew what might happen whilst she was asleep? It was horribly easy for her to imagine herself moving closer to him, seeking his body in her sleep, wanting him, and then waking to find herself touching him.

She drew in a shuddering breath of despair. 'I really don't think that we should share a bed,' she told Ilios carefully.

She could see immediately that he didn't like what she was saying.

'Why not?' Ilios demanded. Had she somehow guessed that she aroused him, despite his determination not to admit that even to himself? Did she think that she was so desirable, so irresistible, and he so weak that he wouldn't be able to stop himself from turning that arousal into something more intimate?

'I just don't think that it would be a good idea,' Lizzie responded, wishing desperately that he would stop pressing her.

'Because you dare to imagine that I might desire you?' Ilios accused her. 'Despite what I have already said about there being no intimacy between us?'

'No,' Lizzie denied immediately. 'It isn't that.'

'Then what is it?'

'I'm afraid I can't say.'

'And I am afraid that you are going to have to—or take the consequences,' Ilios warned her quietly.

Lizzie exhaled very slowly. What he meant was that she was going to have to share his bed unless she came up with a cast-iron reason why she should not do. Her reason might be solid, but her courage certainly wasn't. Of all the unwanted situations she could have had to face, this had to be the worst of them. She was now in a position where she had to defend herself from her own desire for a man who didn't want her by revealing that desire to him. It was her only means of protecting herself from it.

She had never felt more vulnerable or self-conscious, but the truth was that she needed Ilios's help to stop her from making her situation even worse. Once he was aware how she felt, she knew he would take all the steps necessary to ensure temptation was removed out of her way. Desperate situations called for desperate measures, and there was surely no more desperate measure than the one she was going to have to take now. Rather like firefighters tackling a fire that threatened to destroy everything in its path, she was going to have to create a fire-break by deliberately destroying part of her own defences in the hope that doing so would ultimately protect her from herself.

'It isn't *your* desire that worries me,' she told him truthfully, deliberately emphasising the word 'your'.

CHAPTER EIGHT

LIZZIE'S admission was so unexpected, so breathtakingly straightforward and honest, that it took several seconds for Ilios to accept exactly what she had said.

He looked at her, watching the way the colour came and went in her face, seeing the bruised look of misery that shadowed her eyes, and something came to life inside him that he didn't recognise.

Why didn't he say something—anything? Lizzie thought anxiously, even if it was just to reject her.

However, when he did speak it was slowly, spacing out the words.

'Are you trying to tell me that you don't want to share my bed because *you* want *me*?' he asked in disbelief.

Lizzie's throat had gone so tight that it ached with her tension.

'Yes. That is, I think I do. I'm not used to feeling…that is to wanting… I've never actually lusted after anyone before,' she admitted, red-faced.

'"Lusted after"?'

Now Lizzie could see that she had shocked him.

'I'm sorry!' she apologised. 'I didn't want it to happen, but now you can see, can't you, how difficult it would be?

I've really tried not to…to think about it, but sometimes it just sort of overwhelms me. I'm afraid that if we were to share a bed, then… Well, what I mean is I know that you don't want anything to happen between us. I didn't want to have to say anything.'

She gave a small twisted smile, whilst Ilios listened to her with a growing sense of incredulity and disbelief.

'What woman would?' Lizzie continued self-deprecatingly. 'But at least now that you do know, I can rely on you to…to help me…to ensure that—well, that nothing happens.'

Ilios could hardly believe his own ears. Was she really standing there and telling him that she wouldn't share his bed because she was afraid that the sexual temptation of his proximity would be too much for her self-control? Did she really think that he was the kind of man who would allow a *woman* to play the role of hunter in the chase between the sexes? Immediately Ilios wished he had not used such a metaphor, because it had somehow or other caused some very sensual images indeed to break loose inside his imagination—images that were having exactly the opposite effect on him he assumed Lizzie had expected her admission to have.

Her head bowed, Lizzie admitted, 'I know you must be shocked. I was shocked too. That was part of the reason why I didn't want to agree to marry you.'

'You knew then?' Ilios challenged her.

Lizzie swallowed against the painful lump of anguish lodged in her throat. *I knew the minute I saw you,* she could have said. But of course she mustn't.

'I knew that there was something…' she told him carefully. 'But I thought it would go away.'

'And it didn't?'

She shook her head. 'I thought that I could fight against it, that it would be like fighting the hurdles I had to overcome when our parents died, and I will, only at the moment, after tonight and the champagne, I just don't think…'

'So it's only tonight that you don't want to spend in my bed?'

'No, it's not just tonight.'

'So it isn't just the champagne either?'

Lizzie couldn't speak. She couldn't look at him, and she couldn't run from him either. All she could do was simply shake her head.

'I'd be lying if I said that I'd never been propositioned by a woman before, and I'd be lying even more if I said that I'd either welcomed or enjoyed the experience,' Ilios told her abruptly. 'As far as I'm concerned, I'm a man who does his own hunting, who selects the woman he wants and pursues her—not the other way around.'

Lizzie's head came up. 'I wasn't propositioning you,' she denied fiercely. 'I was just trying to explain—to warn you.' When he made no response she continued determinedly, 'I could sleep in the guest room, and then in the morning…'

Ilios was shaking his head.

'No. Now that I am aware of the situation you may rest assured that you can safely leave it to me to take the right steps to deal with it. That was what you wanted, after all, wasn't it? For me to take responsibility for the situation?'

'Yes,' Lizzie was forced to agree.

'Right. I have some work to do—costings to check—and some e-mails to send. So why don't you make yourself at home in what will now be *our* bedroom and stop worrying? It is a husband's duty to protect his wife, is it not?' Ilios's whole manner was dismissive, and indicated that he no longer felt the issue worthy of discussion.

'I'm not your wife—and anyway, a lot of women would take exception to the idea that they might need to be protected,' Lizzie felt bound to point out.

'This is Greece,' Ilios told her firmly. 'And you are both worrying needlessly and imagining problems where none need exist.'

If she did go to bed now, with any luck she would be asleep before Ilios came to join her. In all probability that was why he was staying up to do some work, Lizzie reflected, as she picked up her coat and nodded in acknowledgement of what he had said.

Ilios's bedroom was twice the size of the guest suite, with both a bathroom and a wetroom attached to it. Not that Lizzie allowed herself to spend any more time than was absolutely necessary in the modern bathroom, with its limestone floor and walls, and its huge bowl-shaped bath.

The bed, as Ilios had told her, was very big—wide enough, surely, for two parents and at least four children; plenty wide enough for two adults to sleep in totally separate. Even so, Lizzie looked at the large sofa on the other side of the bedroom and then, still wrapped in her towel, went over to it. One by one she carried the cushions from it over to the bed, where she laid them meticulously down the middle of the immaculate pale grey silk and cotton cover.

There! That should stop her, should she attempt to do anything silly in her sleep.

Now all she had to do was find the cotton pyjamas she had brought with her from home.

Ten minutes later, wearing the tee shirt top and cut-off trousers, Lizzie pulled back the bedclothes and got into 'her' half of the bed.

* * *

Ilios rubbed his hands over his face to ease the tiredness from it and then looked at his watch. Almost two a.m. Lizzie should be asleep by now. Had he really needed to do this? an inner voice scoffed at him. After all, he was perfectly capable of ensuring that nothing happened that he did not want to happen. Wasn't he? Or maybe, given the lengths he was going to to avoid joining her, he wasn't as sure as he'd like to be.

He looked at the sofa. If that was how he felt, then he had better not take any risks, hadn't he? Picking up the cashmere throw that was draped just so over one of the sofas, Ilios lay down with the throw over himself, flicking the remote to switch off the lights.

This was certainly not something he had envisaged when he'd decided that Lizzie would make him a perfect pretend wife, Ilios thought grimly. Sleeping on the sofa whilst she occupied his bed, in order to protect her from herself…

CHAPTER NINE

'COFFEE.'

It was a statement, not a question, and the familiar darkly smoky male voice in which it was delivered brought Lizzie abruptly out of her sleep.

Ilios, dressed in a white towelling bathrobe and smelling discreetly of clean, warm male flesh, was standing beside the bed—her side of the bed—holding out to her a stylish white china mug, obviously wanting her to take it from him. Obediently Lizzie struggled out of her warm cocoon of bedclothes to sit up, reaching for the mug with one hand whilst keeping the bedclothes pressed to her with the other.

'I'm still not safe, then?' Ilios drawled, a gleam of something approaching amusement in the golden eagle eyes that held Lizzie spellbound.

He was actually smiling! Delight flooded through her, causing her to smile back at him before she could stop herself as she took the mug he was holding out to her. Until recollection of their conversation of the night before made Lizzie groan inwardly, and curse whatever had been responsible for her reckless folly.

Unable to come up with a suitably crushing and mature

response, she looked away from him, almost sloshing coffee onto the bedding when she saw that the sofa cushions she had carefully put in place last night had gone.

Her eyes wide with disbelief and censure, she accused Ilios, 'You took the cushions away.'

'I had no other choice. I'm Greek! I have to think what it would do to my reputation as a man if Maria arrived and found that you had barricaded yourself on one side of the bed in isolation.'

'You could have told her that we'd had a quarrel.'

'I could have,' Ilios agreed. 'But there is a saying that you should never sleep with your anger or without your wife. Maria is of the old school, and she would believe that the more intense the quarrel, the more passionate the making up. In Maria's eyes a quarrel between man and wife can result in only one thing—the arrival of a new baby nine months later.'

Lizzie shuddered inwardly and trembled outwardly. Why had he said that? He must know the effect it was likely to have on her after what she had told him. If this was his way of ensuring that she didn't give way to her desire for him, then Lizzie didn't think it was going to work very well.

'There must be something you can say to Maria that would make her accept that we should sleep in separate rooms—after all, we aren't even married yet.'

'No, there is nothing,' Ilios told her. 'You must know that in Greece, especially this part of Greece, a man's maleness is something he must prove to all those who know him in order to win and maintain their respect. That means being the master of his own house. No Greek male would ever publicly admit that his wife's sexual advances were unwelcome.'

'I wasn't suggesting that you that you told her that,' Lizzie informed him indignantly.

Ilios looked down at the bed. Make-up free, with her hair down round her shoulders and the part of her body that wasn't swathed in bedcovers shrouded by what looked like an oversized tee shirt, Lizzie looked nothing like a temptress of any kind. So why was his body telling him in no uncertain terms that she was, and that it was very tempted by her?

Absently glancing around the room, Lizzie noticed something she had not taken in before—the bedding on other side of the bed was pristinely neat. Untouched, in fact.

She turned accusingly to Ilios. 'You didn't sleep with me, did you?'

When his eyebrows rose she corrected herself hastily.

'I mean you didn't sleep in this bed last night.'

'No. I didn't.'

'So where did you sleep, then?'

'On the sofa. It was late when I finished working, and I didn't want to disturb you. You see, you were sleeping on my side of the bed. I could have moved you in your sleep—without waking you, of course—but, given what you had told me, I didn't think it wise to run the risk of you waking up in my arms and thinking...'

'That I'd reached for you in my sleep?' Lizzie guessed.

'Something like that,' Ilios agreed tersely. What he had been going to say was that he hadn't wanted her waking up and thinking that he returned her desire and wanted her. Nor was he going to admit that the thought of holding her in his arms had tormented his body with such a savagely fierce sexual ache for her through the long, slow hours of the night that he hadn't been able to sleep.

'I've been thinking that perhaps we should just be engaged. Not actually get married. And then—well, you could tell Maria that I'm not the kind of woman who shares a bed with her husband before he is her husband,' Lizzie told Ilios.

'I need a wife, not a fiancée. You know that. And besides, it's too late.'

'Too late?' Lizzie's heart had started to thump uncomfortably heavily. 'What do you mean?'

'We've got an appointment at eleven-thirty this morning with the notary who has arranged all the paperwork for our wedding. He will accompany us to the town hall, so that the formalities can be finalized, and then we can be married.'

'Today? So soon? But surely that isn't possible? I mean, doesn't it take longer than that to arrange things?'

'Normally speaking, yes, but when I explained to my friends at the town hall how impatient I am to make you my wife, they very kindly speeded things up for us. Manos Construction is currently contracted to do some refurbishment work on certain parts of the city, and the local government is keen to get that work finished ahead of schedule.'

'You mean you bribed them into making it possible for us to get married so quickly?' Lizzie accused him.

'No, I did not "bribe" them, as you put it.' Anger flashed in Ilios's eyes. 'I do not conduct my business by way of bribes—I thought I had already made that clear to you. All I did was agree to do what I could to ensure the contract is finished ahead of time and to the highest standard. Something I always insist on. We are subject to earthquakes here. It is always important that this is taken into account on construction projects, although some less than scrupulous contractors do try to cut corners. Now, I shall get dressed whilst you finish your coffee, and then leave you in peace to get dressed yourself.'

* * *

Peace? How was it possible for her to have anything remotely approaching peace now that she had met Ilios? Lizzie asked herself grimly just over an hour later, when she stood in the dressing room she was now sharing with her soon-to-be husband, studying her own reflection.

She was wearing an off-white wool dress with a bubble skirt and a neat boxy matching jacket—the nearest thing she had been able to find amongst her new clothes that looked anything like 'bridal'. Not that this was a proper wedding, or she a proper bride, of course. She must remember that. She was hardly likely to forget it, was she? It had been a shock to learn that they were getting married so quickly, but she suspected that she should have guessed Ilios wouldn't want to waste any time putting his plans into practice.

She walked towards the door. It was a strange feeling to know that the next time she looked at her reflection in this mirror she would not be Lizzie Wareham any more. She would be Mrs Ilios Manos.

CHAPTER TEN

'REMEMBER that you agreed to this,' Ilios warned Lizzie as they stood together on the steps leading of the town hall.

Ilios's notary, who had been with them the whole time whilst the simple ceremony making them man and wife had been taking place, stood back discreetly as Ilios took her arm.

Not trusting herself to speak, Lizzie nodded her head and forced a brief tight smile. It was all very well telling herself that it wasn't a real marriage, nor a proper wedding, nor Ilios her real husband—there had still been that dreadful moment when they had stood together before the official marrying them and inside her head she had seen the small church in the village where she had grown up, and herself dressed in white, with her father standing proudly at her side, her mother fussing over her dress and her sisters laughing, Ilios watching them smiling, and she had felt a tearing, aching sense of loss strike her right to her heart.

'Come,' Ilios urged her.

The sun was shining, drying pavements still wet from the rain that had fallen whilst they were inside the building, and the breeze was cool. Summer, with its heat, was still many weeks away, and for the first time since she had agreed to marry Ilios Lizzie longed desperately for those weeks to fly past, so that she would be free to go home to her family. It had felt so wrong, so lonely getting married without them—even if it was a pretend marriage—and she ached with nostalgia for her childhood and homesickness for her sisters and the twins.

The sunlight shone brightly on the newness of her wedding ring. She must stop feeling sorry for herself and remember why she had agreed to marry Ilios, she told herself—why she had *had* to marry him. He was still cupping her elbow, very much the attentive bridegroom—no doubt for the benefit of the notary to whom he was now speaking in Greek. Both of them were looking at her, their conversation excluding her, reminding her that she was an outsider in a foreign land and very much alone.

The pressure of Ilios's hold on her arm urged her closer to him, as though…as though he had somehow sensed what she was feeling and wanted to reassure her—just as a real husband would have done. That, of course, was ridiculous. Even if he *had* guessed how she was feeling he was hardly likely to care, was he? She could feel his thumb lightly rubbing her skin through her jacket. He was probably so used to caressing his lovers that he didn't even realise what he was doing, Lizzie thought waspishly, as she tried to ignore the effect his absent-minded caress was having on her body. He was turning towards her, smiling warmly at her—a false smile, for his audience, of course.

'Forgive us for speaking in Greek, *agapi mou*,' he told her. 'We were just discussing some business. But now, Nikos, I am impatient to take my beautiful wife for a celebratory lunch.'

The notary had soon gone, and Ilios was handing her back into his car.

Lizzie had assumed that Ilios would take her straight back to the apartment, and leave her to go on to his office, but instead he parked the car in a convenient space outside an elegant-looking restaurant.

'I didn't think you were serious about us celebrating,' Lizzie told him.

'I wasn't—but we do have to eat,' he pointed out dismissively, before getting out of the car and coming round to her door to open it for her.

They might not be publicly celebrating their marriage, but the keen-eyed restaurant owner who had greeted Ilios so warmly on their arrival must have noticed something— her new wedding ring, perhaps? Lizzie acknowledged. Her heart sank as he approached their table now, with a beaming smile and champagne. Of course she couldn't possibly offend him by refusing to accept his kindness, but even so she couldn't help glancing at Ilios as their glasses were filled with the sparkling liquid.

She wished that she hadn't when he lifted his glass towards her own and said softly, and very meaningfully, 'To us.'

'To us,' Lizzie echoed weakly, quickly sipping her own drink to disguise the fact that her hand was trembling. She mustn't blame herself too much for her reaction, Lizzie tried to comfort herself. After all a marriage, even a pretend marriage, was bound to have some effect on a person's emotions—just as a man like Ilios was bound to have an effect on a woman's awareness of her own sexuality.

The toast didn't have to be taken as a toast to them as a couple, and she was sure the deliberate emphasis Ilios had put on it was a private reminder to her that he was toasting them as separate individuals rather than a couple in their newly official union.

She found that even though she had been hungry her emotions were now too stirred up for her to have much appetite for the delicious food. Desperate for something to distract her from her unwanted and growing awareness that, no matter how illogical it might be, the fact that she and Ilios were married had produced within her an unexpected feeling of commitment to him—a sort of protective, deeply female need to reach out to him and heal the damage that had been done to his emotions and his life— Lizzie glanced round the restaurant.

Her attention focussed on a family group at another table. The parents, a pretty dark-haired young mother and a smiling paternalistic-looking father, were accompanied by three children: a little boy who looked slightly older than the twins, a girl who Lizzie guessed must be about four, and what was obviously a fairly new baby in a car seat buggy combo drawn up to the table. Although the children were not all the same sex, the relationship between them reminded her of her own childhood. The little boy, serious-looking and obviously proud of his seniority, was keeping an older-brotherly eye on the little girl and the baby, whilst the little girl was leaning over the buggy, cooing at the baby. Over their heads the parents exchanged amused and tender smiles.

Hastily Lizzie reached for her champagne, to try and swallow back the huge lump of aching emotion forming in her throat. Not for herself—she and her sisters had experienced the kind of love she could see emanating from this family. No, her sadness and pain was for those other children—Ilios's sons.

Before she could change her mind she asked Ilios, 'Are

you sure there isn't some way that you and your cousin could mend the broken fences between you and get your relationship on a happier footing?'

'If that's a roundabout way of trying to tell me that you're anxious to bring our marriage to an end as soon as possible, then—'

'No, it isn't that.' Lizzie stopped him. 'It's the children—*your* children,' she emphasized, when she saw Ilios look frowningly towards the table she had been studying.

Leaning across the table, she asked him quietly, 'Have you thought about what might happen to them if anything were to happen to you? They'd have no one—no father, no mother, obviously, no family Ilios. No one in their lives to give them a sense of continuity and security and…and… They would have no one to tell them their history, no one to tell them about you. I know that financially they would be protected, but that isn't enough. They'd be dreadfully alone.'

Ilios was looking down at his plate. She had infuriated him, Lizzie expected, and no doubt he was going to tell her that the future of his sons was none of her business.

When he did lift his head and look at her Lizzie found it impossible to gauge what he was thinking from his grim expression.

'So you think that I should—what was the phrase you used?—"mend fences" with my cousin so that in the eventuality of my unexpected demise he will open his arms and his heart to my sons and become a second father to them?'

Put like that, what she had said did sound rather like something out of a sentimental film, Lizzie admitted.

'Family is important.' She insisted.

'What if I were to do as you suggest and my sons ended

up being humiliated and tormented by my cousin, just as I was myself? What if he abused the trust I placed in him for his own financial benefit?'

'That's what I meant about wondering if it was possible for you to mend fences with him,' Lizzie defended herself. 'Now, before it's too late.'

'I see. I become reconciled with my cousin, and you get a quick escape from a commitment and an agreement you're obviously already wanting to renege on?'

'No! I am prepared to stay married to you for as long as it takes.'

Ilios arched one eyebrow in a silent but unmistakably mocking query, and then asked her softly, 'As long as what takes?'

Lizzie felt like stamping her foot. Ignoring her own feeling of self-consciousness, she told him fiercely, 'You know perfectly well what I was trying to say. I am not attempting to renege on our agreement. If I did that you'd be within your moral rights to demand repayment of the money you gave me—money I need to ensure my family's financial security. I know you've said that you don't believe in love, but to deny your own sons the emotional protection they will need...' She hesitated, and then decided to ignore her anxiety about angering him. If she was to be his children's champion then she must do so without considering her own position. 'Surely you can't want them to suffer in their childhood as you did?'

Ilios looked at her in silence, whilst she held her breath—waiting for his response.

When it came, it was both unexpected and underhanded.

'Obviously it isn't only sexual lust for my body that champagne arouses in you, but a lust for plain speaking.'

'What I said doesn't have anything to do with me drinking champagne,' she said vehemently.

'No? Don't the words *in vino veritas* mean anything to you?'

In wine there is truth. But it wasn't the champagne that had loosened her inhibitions. It was seeing that small happy family. Only somehow Lizzie didn't think that Ilios would believe her—no matter how much she tried to correct his interpretation of the situation.

Mend fences with his cousin? Ilios thought grimly of the way Tino had deliberately tormented him as a child—the way he had taunted him by pointing out that he had a mother, aunts and uncles and cousins, whilst Ilios's own mother had hated him so much she had abandoned him. Of course Tino had had his own cross to bear. Their grandfather had never let him forget that his father had died a coward.

To their grandfather male descendants had simply been there to fulfil and continue the Manos destiny: to own Villa Manos, the land on which it stood, and continue their once proud history. Nothing and no one else mattered.

But Lizzie had had a point. No man was immortal, and if he *should* die before his sons were old enough to manage their own affairs there would be plenty of vultures waiting to pick at the vulnerable flesh of their inheritance.

He and Lizzie looked at life and humankind from opposite viewpoints. She believed passionately in the power of love, in parenthood and families. He did not. When called upon to do so she had put her siblings first, and every word she spoke about them showed that she would do anything and everything she could to safeguard and protect them. Just as she would her children, should she become a mother? Ilios frowned. That did not accord with his own beliefs about her sex. He could concede that Lizzie might be that one rare exception. But so what?

The trouble was there were beginning to be far too

many *so whats* in his reactions to Lizzie Wareham, Ilios acknowledged, remembering that he had asked himself the same question when he had been forced to admit that he was sexually aware of her—sexually aware of her and aroused by her presence. He had no rational explanation for the way she made him think and feel, and trying to find one only served to increase his awareness of the effect she was having on him and his desire to crush it.

And yet, as much as he wanted to impose his will on his awareness of her, his body refused to accept it. Quite the opposite in fact. The ache that had been tormenting him flared from a dull presence to a sharp, predatory male clamour. Totally against what he had believed he knew about himself, her admission of desire for him had increased his own desire for her rather than destroy it. Increased it, enhanced it, and made him want her with a suddenly very driven intensity that he had never experienced before.

Ilios looked at Lizzie's half-empty glass of champagne, and then at the bottle still in the ice bucket. Picking it up, he told her, 'You'd better finish this, otherwise we'll offend Spiros—and I don't want to end up never being able to get a table here again.'

Lizzie shook her head.

'I've already had one full glass,' she reminded him.

'And two might turn your thoughts to your uncontrollable lust for my body and a whole catalogue of things you'd like to do to it?' he taunted her.

Before Lizzie could formulate a suitable crushing response he continued easily, as he filled her glass, 'It seems to me that the best way to quench your sexual curiosity would be to satisfy it.'

What the hell had made him say that? Ilios challenged

himself grimly. But of course he already knew the answer. Lizzie wasn't the only one battling against a desire she didn't want. Maybe what he'd suggested was the best way for them both to rid themselves of a need that neither of them wished to have.

What was happening? Was she hallucinating or was Ilios actually suggesting…? No, she must be imagining it.

'Is…is that an offer?' she managed to ask Ilios, in what she hoped was a voice that suggested she knew it wasn't.

Only she was left thoroughly bemused at his response.

'If you want it to be.'

Did she? What was happening here? Was Ilios really implying that he wanted her? Physically? Sexually? In bed?

Lizzie refused to answer him. She simply didn't dare.

She didn't like the way Ilios was looking at her. And she certainly didn't like the way that look was making tiny rivulets of giddy excitement and longing rush through her body, like teenage fans rushing towards an idol, oblivious to reality or danger. Neither did she like the way she suddenly and overpoweringly wanted to look at Ilios's mouth and imagine… She could hardly breathe, barely think—at least not of anything that didn't involve her getting up close and personal with Ilios and discovering if that full bottom lip did mean what it was supposed to mean. What would happen were she to touch it with her fingertips, taste it with her tongue, explore it and…?

In desperation Lizzie took what she hoped would be a cooling gulp of her champagne. She certainly needed something to dampen down the sensual heat that had taken hold of her. Ilios was still looking at her—looking at her as though he knew every word she was thinking and every thing she was feeling. No, she did not like that look and all it suggested at all. Lizzie drew in a shaky breath of air as her conscience prodded her. Well, all right, she did like it—but she didn't like the fact that she liked it.

The truth was, Lizzie realised ten minutes later, as Ilios held opened the car door for her, that much as she ached for the experience of having sex with Ilios, and eager as she was to explore and appreciate every bit of him, she was still female enough to want *him* to make the first move and show her that he wanted her as much as if not more than she wanted him. She needed to know his desire for her. She needed to feel that he wanted her so much that he could not deny that wanting. Only then would she truly be able to indulge her own desire for him. And of course that was not going to happen—was it?

But what if it did? Ilios could be right, and the best way for her to get over the longing that was tormenting her *was* for her to go to bed with him. Hot excitement kicked through her body. She was a woman, she reminded herself—she was twenty-seven years old, after all—not a teenager. She knew perfectly well what the situation was and she couldn't claim any different. Did she really want to go back home without experiencing what Ilios offered her just because she had panicked and wanted to be wooed? Wouldn't she, years from now, look back in regret, or even worse in yearning, for what she had not had? It was perfectly safe, after all, and so was she. It wasn't as though she was in love with Ilios and thought that somehow having sex with him—making love with him—was going to change him and cause him to fall head over heels in love with her.

No, this was purely about sexual desire. It was about answering, exploring, satisfying the need that had been aching, growing inside her from their first meeting. No one but the two of them need ever know that she had briefly stepped out of the role she had cast for herself after the death of her parents—a role that meant that she must always be the responsible eldest sister, monitoring her own behaviour in order that she could set their family standards and guide her younger siblings. Here, with Ilios, it was safe for her to experience being what in her real life she could never be—sensually eager, responsive to her own desires and those of her partner, without having to think about anything or anyone else.

What possible harm could there be in it? If it happened it would be a one-off, that was all—an exciting, tantalising sensual adventure. If Ilios should repeat his offer, was she going to be brave enough to do what she knew she wanted to do? Or was she going to be a coward who would spend the rest of her life regretting her hesitation?

CHAPTER ELEVEN

THEY'D travelled back to the Manos Corporation building in silence, and in that same silence they had got out of the car and travelled in the lift to where they were now—outside the door to the apartment, with Ilios unlocking it.

'What's this?' Lizzie asked curiously, almost forgetting the reason for her earlier inability to speak as she bent down to pick up the small blue bead lying on the floor just inside the door.

'Maria's obviously been in, and equally obviously she must know the wedding was today,' Ilios answered, taking the bead from her and putting it back down on the floor. 'It's meant to ward off the evil eye—a Greek tradition that involves those who have something to protect doing so by means of the gift of one of these. Maria obviously approves of our marriage, and by leaving this is protecting it and us from bad luck.'

Lizzie nodded her head. She'd have liked to have changed out of her white wool dress and coat into something less high-maintenance, but she was concerned that any move towards the bedroom on her part might be wrongly interpreted by Ilios.

'Who designed the garden?' she asked him instead. 'I haven't been out in it yet, but—'

'I designed it. Or at least I copied certain elements of the gardens at Villa Manos and adapted them for here.'

Whilst they were talking they'd walked into the living room.

'Will I be safe if I offer you a walk round the garden?' Ilios asked.

Did he really think she would pounce on him? Was he expecting her to make all the running? She couldn't, Lizzie knew. Not without knowing that he wanted her too.

Lizzie wondered what he was really thinking—and feeling. Had he meant what he'd said in the restaurant, or had he simply been amusing himself at her expense? Even worse, had he actually been thinking about taking her to bed and then decided upon reflection not to bother? Maybe she had misunderstood what he'd said, or taken it too seriously, and now he was stepping back from that conversation because he hadn't meant it. Lizzie's face burned at the thought.

'If you don't mind my saying so, if you would like to see the garden you may want to think about getting changed first, into something less…'

The sound of Ilios's voice focussed her attention on what he was saying, and valiantly Lizzie tried to put her mixed-up feelings to one side and focus instead of reality.

'Something less white?' she offered brightly. She refused to use the word *bridal*, with all that it implied.

Ilios nodded his head.

'Look, I've got a couple of e-mails I need to send, so why don't you go and get changed? Take as long as you wish. There's no rush.'

* * *

If Ilios had actually known how uncomfortable she'd been feeling, both in her outfit and about saying she wanted to change out of it, and had wanted to put her at her ease, he couldn't have done so more effectively, Lizzie acknowledged several minutes later, as she stood beneath the shower in the bathroom off the master bedroom. Not that she imagined he *could* have known how she was feeling. In fact he had probably simply wanted her out of the way. The more she thought about it, the more she thought she had been a complete fool for thinking he had been suggesting that he wanted her.

She showered quickly, using her own favourite shower gel from Jo Malone, and noting as she did so that the container was almost empty. Jo Malone treats were something she wasn't going to be able to indulge in any more. No doubt the whole family would end up using something safe and suitable for the twins. Smiling to herself, Lizzie stepped out of the shower, drying herself speedily and then wrapping a towel sarong-wise round her body. Removing the cap she had put on her head to keep her hair dry, she opened the door to the dressing room and came to an abrupt halt almost in mid-step, her eyes widening as she saw Ilios opening his wardrobe. Like her, he had quite obviously taken a shower—only his towel sat low on his hips and finished midway down his thigh.

Her 'Oh!' was a soft, half-choked sound as betraying as the manner in which she clutched her towel protectively to her body. 'I thought you said you were going to be busy sending e-mails,' was all she could think of to say.

'I changed my mind and decided to have a shower instead.' He wasn't going to tell her that the ache she had induced within his body had made it impossible for him to do anything other than give in to the need to take a cold shower.

He must have used the guest room—which, of course, was why he was here right now, looking for his clothes.

'I'll…I'll wait in the bathroom until…until you've finished.'

Was that squeaky, nervous voice really her own?

'So that you aren't overwhelmed by your desire for me?'

Why had she ever said that to him about being concerned that she might be the one overcome with lust? Both the joke and her sense of humour were becoming stretched to breaking point.

'I'll tell you what…' Ilios's voice was muffled by the wardrobe door that he had opened between them, and Lizzie had to strain to hear what he was saying. Automatically she took a couple of steps towards him, so that she could hear properly.

What would he tell her?

'Instead of talking about your desire for me, why don't you come here and show me?'

The door swung closed. Ilios was standing far too close to her—or rather she was standing far too close to him. But even as she decided to step back his right hand curled into her towel and tugged—firmly.

What was she going to do? If she stayed where she was she would be in danger of losing her towel, and if she moved it would have to be forward, towards him, and that would mean…

'Nothing to say?'

She was up close against him, and his hand wasn't gripping her towel. Instead it was smoothing its way up her bare arm and over her shoulder, stroking her neck, cupping her face. One hand, and then both.

'Very well, then, why don't I do this instead?'

He finished his sentence in a whisper, practically forming the words against her lips with his lips—lips that were smooth and warm and expertly knowing as they moved slowly over hers, pausing, lifting to allow her to gasp in a shaken breath. His fingers smoothed the skin of her face, and then he was kissing her again, slowly and lingeringly, each second of his touch its own intimate world of pleasure, given and then removed. A tantalising, tormenting unbelievably erotic pleasure, nothing more than light skimming kisses but at the same time so deeply sensual that they transported her to a whole new world.

Each time he kissed her and then withdrew Lizzie moved closer, hungering for more. Her own hand lifted to his face.

'I've wanted to do this from the first moment I saw you,' she admitted breathlessly, touching his skin with her fingertips, absorbing its texture, learning the shape of the muscles that lay beneath the warm flesh, her eyes dark and hot with what she was feeling.

'Only this? Nothing more?'

Ilios's voice was as soft and warm, as erotic to her senses as the dark cross of fine silky hair that painted his body. His words, with their tempting invitation, made her tremble beneath the intensity of her own desire.

'Not this, perhaps?' he suggested, sliding his hand round the curve of her throat and kissing her bare shoulder, each movement of his lips setting off a firestorm of quivering delight.

'Or this?' His tongue stroked the sensitive flesh just behind her earlobe, making her shudder visibly and cling to him as though her flesh was so boneless and pliable that she could melt into him. She wanted him so much—which made it all the harder to bear when he stopped kissing her and released her.

That was it? He was going to leave her like this? Aching so badly for him that—

'Come on,' he told her. 'I'll show you the garden.'

The garden? Now? She didn't want the garden. She wanted him. But Ilios was reaching for her hand and drawing her with him as he headed for the door.

They had been late coming back from lunch, and now it was almost dark. Cleverly placed lights illuminated the garden, transforming it into a space filled with magical images. The ruined temple was highlighted against the evening sky, the colonnade woven with a net of tiny starry lights.

'It looks very pretty,' Lizzie admitted absently, still dazed by his kisses, and still wearing nothing more than the towel wrapped around her. It was true about the garden, but they were now in a bedroom that possessed a very large bed, and right now all she wanted was to be lying on that bed with Ilios, with nothing to come between them, or to come between her and her increasingly urgent need to explore every bit of him.

Ilios obviously didn't feel the same way, because he was leading her down a smooth path, the tiles cool beneath her bare feet. The raised walls protecting the garden made it pleasantly warm, and above them the evening sky was studded with stars like diamonds in velvet, their gleam reflected in the swimming pool.

It would have been on nights such as these that the gods came down from Olympus to mingle with mortal men—and women, Lizzie thought, remembering how some of the Greek myths involved human women being impregnated by handsome gods. She paused to touch the leaves of a small olive tree set into a tub.

'Olives and vines. Food and drink,' Ilios murmured.

'Ambrosia and nectar,' Lizzie whispered back.

They had reached the side of the swimming pool, and as she looked back at the ruin Ilios spoke teasingly.

'I think we can dispense with these, don't you?'

Lizzie sucked in her breath as he plucked away her towel, but the self-consciousness she had expected to feel was banished—melting away, she suspected, in the heat that filled her as his gaze stroked over every bit of her, just as though he was actually caressing her.

What was happening to her? She was with a man who made her feel as no man had ever made her feel before, and it was the most extraordinary, the most deliciously sensual and exciting feeling she had ever had. Her awareness of her own nakedness actually gave her an additional frisson of pleasure, made her want to stretch erotically beneath the warmth of Ilios's gaze. She watched as he removed his own towel, her heart thudding into a climax of fierce female anticipation as she waited for him to take her in his arms.

Instead he dived into the water, slicing it cleanly and surfacing a few feet out into the pool before turning to hold out his arms to her.

'Jump in. The water's warm.'

They were going for a *swim*?

Lizzie took a deep breath and jumped.

Ilios's arms closed round her. They were standing body to body, the water just covering her breasts. It lapped against them, a warm touch against her sensitised nipples and between her legs, as sensual as a lover's touch gently caressing her. Ilios's hands stroked over her skin, his movements vibrating in the water so that it felt as though he and the water were one. He had complete mastery over her desire, arousing it, compelling it, filling her with pleasure and then drawing it from her. Her body was a willing vessel, to be filled with the pleasure he was giving her. The sensation of his breath against her skin made her cry out softly, arching her throat to its touch just as she was arching her body to his possession. She was his to do with as he pleased—to give her all the sensual delight he was giving her.

Lizzie closed her eyes beneath the onslaught of the sweet agony of growing need, opening them quickly when Ilios moved to float onto his back, taking her with him so that she was lying on top of him, supported by him, her body pressing into his, every inch of her skin aware of every inch of his, where they touched and where they didn't.

He kicked out strongly through the water, his hands sliding down her back and then up again slowly, stroking her skin with his fingertips, moving lower with each caress.

Lizzie held her breath against the fever of her own longing. Only when he finally stroked past her hips to cup her buttocks was she able to exhale in shaky relief. Now, at last, against her own sex she could feel his, solid with muscle and arousal, pressing up against her as Ilios pressed her down against himself.

Within her the heat of her own desire seemed to be melting her flesh, so that it softened and expanded. Her body moved under his hands and their grip on her tightened. It couldn't be happening like this, without any need for anything other than the satisfaction of the compulsive drive that was now pounding through her, but it was. All she could think of—all she wanted—was the satisfaction of having the full deep thrust of him within her.

Ilios was like a mythical god, Lizzie thought dizzily. His

touch made reality and reason disappear and replaced them with the most ancient and relentless of human drives. The need he aroused in her possessed her and drove her, so that all she wanted was to wrap herself around him.

They had reached the far end of the pool, where water fell from the top of a cliff past the opening to a grotto with soft lighting that turned the water a rich blue-green.

When Ilios eased her away from his body and stood up Lizzie could see that the water here was shallower. Water from the pool ran down his body, and Lizzie's gaze followed each drop hungrily.

'What?' Ilios asked watching her gaze with his own. 'What is it you want to do? This?'

He leaned forward and held her waist, kissing his way down past her collarbone and between her breasts—light, lingering kisses accompanied by the curling movement of his tongue against her damp flesh, making her burn with longing to do the same to him. His hand dropped to her thighs. Lizzie gave a small moan that became a gasp of tortured pleasure when Ilios started to kiss the slope of her breast, and then to circle the tight ache of her nipple with his tongue-tip.

The heavy pulse of the ache low down in her body picked up tempo. She leaned into Ilios's hold, her thighs parting. In response he tongued her nipple, and then drew it between his lips. Wanting more, Lizzie pushed towards him, welcoming the heat of his hand between her legs, whimpering with pleasure when his fingers found her wetness, her body clamouring for urgent and immediate release.

But instead Ilios lifted her out of the water and put her down at the side of the pool, then getting out himself to join her. Lizzie's heart was thudding. Her body was aching with frustration at the interruption and the removal of his pleasure-giving touch.

She reached for him, wanting to show him how she felt, cupping his face as he had cupped her own earlier, and then kissing him fiercely and eagerly, arching her body into his. His arms tightened round her and he kissed her back.

'We need to go back inside,' he told her. His voice was thick with the desire she shared as he urged her towards the bedroom.

'I know,' she whispered back. 'But I don't want to let you go. I want you so much.' She kissed him again, her hands on his body, her own body on fire with all that she was feeling.

Somehow, between increasingly passionate kisses, they managed to make it to the bedroom, where Lizzie wrapped her arms tightly around Ilios and kissed him, tasting his mouth with her own. She smoothed her hands over his shoulders and his back, stoking the heat of her own arousal with every caress as her senses greedily absorbed the pleasure of their intimacy. Every bit of him was hers to explore and enjoy, and her fingertips memorised the smooth flesh at the back of his neck, the thick strength of his dark hair, the shape of his ears, whilst her senses recorded his response to her touch: the way he arched his head back into her hold, the small thick sound of pleasure he made when she caressed the tender flesh behind his ear, the accelerated sound of his breathing when she had kissed his skin. Small milestones on the longer journey they were sharing, each one faithfully monitored and logged within her heart.

Her *heart*? But that would mean… From the shocked thud of her heartbeat its reverberations spread out through her, carrying to every part of her body and mind a warning—a message of anxiety and apprehension laced with disbelief. Surely there was only one reason why her heart might want to log every second of her intimacy with Ilios? If her heart was involved, then so were her emotions. Emotions and Ilios did not and could not mix. They were incompatible. Just as she and Ilios were incompatible.

Lizzie turned to him, but before she could even think of what she might reasonably say to bring an end to something she knew now would put her in emotional danger, Ilios was scooping her up, carrying her over to the bed, and kissing her with such shocking sensuality as he placed her on it that he immediately awakened her previous urgent desire.

In its fierce clamour it was impossible for her to hear any other voice—impossible for her to think of anything other than the growing sensual tension possessing her body.

Leaning over her, Ilios caressed her body, lingering over each touch with a focussed intensity that was all by itself unbearably erotic, driving her to reach for him. His lips brushed hers; his hand brushed her sex. His tongue-tip parted her lips whilst his hand parted her thighs.

Lizzie could feel her heart hammering into her ribs. Supporting himself with his other hand on the bed, Ilios watched her face as he touched her slowly and intimately, until she was opening helplessly to him, arching up to him for more.

'I want you. I want you, Ilios. Now—please.'

Lizzie's words, gasped in eager longing, pierced Ilios's hot desire, chiming a warning within himself that automatically set off his own protective defences. He had no means of ensuring that their intimacy would be safe. From what Lizzie had told him he doubted that she used any form of contraception as an automatic course. The thought of the health of either of them being affected by them having sex was one he dismissed immediately. He had never taken any risks with his sexual health, and he doubted that Lizzie had had enough previous sexual experience to have risked her own. But they were not protected against unwanted pregnancy, and that meant that he should stop—right now. After all, he had his future planned—and the children that would be a part of it. His children—his sons—protected from the pain he had known as a child, protected from any mother who might reject them or subject him to her avaricious financial demands.

His children who, according to Lizzie, having been conceived in the sterile atmosphere of a laboratory and carried by a woman they would never know, would be deprived of love.

'Ilios?'

Lizzie reached up and touched his face, not understanding why he wasn't responding to her, stroking her fingertips along the length of his sweat-dampened torso, trailing the narrow line of dark hair across his flat belly.

The look of hungry and absorbed need the moonlight revealed in her expression re-ignited the desire Ilios had been trying to suppress. Like flames devouring dry timber it raced through him, overpowering everything that tried to stand in its way, including his own inner warning voice. His body moved of its own accord, his mind powerless to control its need. And Lizzie reached for him, drawing him down towards her, her lips parting in the same longing he could feel in the way she moved to welcome him between her thighs.

The first hot, slick, sweet taste of her sex against his own brought down what was left of his self-control as effectively as a tidal wave smashing down a sandcastle on the beach.

He was within her, taking her, giving to her as they began the swift surging climb towards immortality. On the journey there were brief seconds of time when the pleasure was so intense, like stars within reach on a journey to the moon, that Lizzie was almost distracted enough to want to reach out to them—but then the drive of Ilios's body within her own reminded her of the greater purpose, their ultimate shared destination.

It came for her with convulsive tightening of her body that quickened into her orgasm, just as she felt Ilios's surrender to its fierce embrace spilling hotly into her.

Into her? Like an annoying fly, intruding on the wonderful peace of a lazy summer afternoon, the two words buzzed agitatedly inside her head, ignoring Lizzie's attempts to brush them away so that she could enjoy the pure heaven of lying fulfilled and sweetly aching in the aftermath of orgasm in Ilios's arms.

They hadn't used any contraception. It might not be true that having sex standing up prevented pregnancy, but perhaps if she got up instead of lying there… She was a responsible adult, after all, and there was no place in her life for an unplanned pregnancy.

So why, instead of doing something, or even saying something, was she instead luxuriating in lying close to Ilios, her hand on his chest, registering the beat of his heart gradually returning to normal? Her fingers played with the soft damp hair on his chest, and she enjoyed the male possessiveness of the leg he had thrown across her own, as though wanting to keep her as close to him as she wanted him to be close to her.

Ilios was leaning over her, his hand on her neck, his fingers stroking her skin.

'Good?' he asked.

'Heaven,' Lizzie responded truthfully. 'Absolutely heaven.'

Ilios gathered her close, ignoring the inner voice that was warning him he had just done something that broke all his rules, and something he was going to regret.

CHAPTER TWELVE

'I'VE got to go out to the villa today, to meet with one of the contractors, and I wondered if you'd like to come with me?'

The sudden frown that followed Ilios's invitation made Lizzie wonder if he had spoken without thinking and was now regretting having done so. But, faced with the prospect of another day on her own, sightseeing in the city, when she could instead see the house that had such a fascinating history, she was not going to ask Ilios if he would like to withdraw his invitation.

'I'd love to,' she told him truthfully. After all, it wasn't just Villa Manos she would get to see properly. She would also be with Ilios. Her heart leapt even as her thoughts filled her with guilt.

It had been disquieting to wake in Ilios's arms in the early hours of the morning after they had made love—several days ago now. She'd known that she had crossed a barrier she had never intended to cross. Lying with her head on Ilios's chest, listening to the sound of his breathing, Lizzie had been forced to admit to herself what she had recognised earlier in the evening. Somehow emotion had become entangled in what she had truthfully believed to be merely physical desire. And that emotion was love. An emotion Ilios had already told her he did not want in his life.

But that was all right, she assured herself determinedly now. After all, she was not going to tell him about her love for him. She wasn't going to offer it to him. She wasn't going to do anything different because of it. When the time came she would still pack up her belongings, fold her love in tissue paper in her memory, and take it with her. It was hers, and if she wished to cherish it and protect it, and every now and again remove it from the place where she had hidden it to relive those memories she had made, then that was her business—wasn't it? She was mature enough not to allow it to intrude into what was in reality a business relationship, a business commitment. Ilios had paid her— not to sleep with him of course, but to marry him. In doing so she was providing him a means of outmanoeuvring his cousin, and preventing him from causing him difficulties and delays with regard to their grandfather's will.

What on earth had made him ask Lizzie for her company? Ilios didn't know—or rather he was determined not to know, because of what knowing the answer to his own question might mean.

The night he had taken her to bed had changed everything between them. And it had also changed him. Ilios knew that there were those who came into contact with him who considered him hard and demanding, but the demands he made on others, the expectations he had of them, were nothing compared with those he made on and had for himself.

In taking Lizzie to bed in the first place he had broken his own rules, and that was bad enough. However, even though he had known they were not using contraception he had still gone ahead—and it was that fact that most challenged his perceptions of himself. He could have stopped. His mind had given him a warning that had in turn given him the opportunity to stop. But he had ignored that warning. Why? Because at that point he had been too aroused to want to stop? He was thirty-six years old, dammit, not a teenager and he knew it. Now it was that knowledge that was rubbing a raw place inside his head. Like grit in a shoe, demanding attention, a question that wanted an answer.

Why, when he had been aware of what he was doing and the risk he was taking, and when he had had the opportunity to stop, had he not done so? Why had he, in fact, deliberately continued? Knowing what might result? His life was planned out—his way ahead clear. Impregnating Lizzie with his child was not part of that plan, and neither that child nor Lizzie herself had any place in his future.

And now, when surely he ought to be distancing himself from Lizzie, he had actually invited her to spend the day with him.

It would be both heaven and hell to spend the day with Ilios, Lizzie knew. What had happened to her determination to fight what was happening to her? She would recover it, she assured herself. But just for today she was going to allow herself to bask inwardly in the happiness she felt and the delight of being with him. Inwardly. Outwardly, of course, she must treat the day and Ilios himself in exactly the same way she would have done an appointment with any client she might be accompanying, to view a property they wanted her to restyle for them. All right, so Ilios wasn't going to be asking her to restyle Villa Manos, and for her own sake she must remember why he had married her. As soon as Ilios deemed that their marriage had served its purpose she would be on her way home, and their marriage would be brought to an end.

With that in mind, when she joined him in the living room half an hour after they had finished breakfast, she was wearing her 'professional uniform' of jeans and a white tee shirt—although the new jeans were part of her Mrs Manos wardrobe and were designer. They fitted her perfectly, just like the tee shirt. She carried a jacket over her arm.

Like her, Ilios was also casually dressed in jeans. When he turned his back on her to place his coffee mug in the dishwasher Lizzie had an excellent view of the way in which the denim fitted the muscular firmness of his buttocks, and shamefully she could feel her heartbeat increasing as her gaze lingered on him longer than it should have done. Her? Ogling a man's body? Since when? But Ilios was no ordinary man, was he? He was the man she loved. And the temptation to go up to him and lean against him, hoping that he would turn round and take her in his arms, was almost overwhelming.

It didn't help that Ilios was now coming to bed after she had fallen asleep and getting up in the morning before she was awake, making it very plain that he did not want a repetition of the intimacy they had shared. Although the one good thing about her discovering that she loved him was that she did not now need to fear being overcome by her lust—knowing that she loved him had changed everything. It meant that she would not and could not risk Ilios recognising how she felt.

Pinning a bright, businesslike smile to her face, she asked Ilios conversationally, 'Is the interior of Villa Manos modelled on Villa Emo as well as the exterior?'

This was another unfamiliar issue he was having to deal with, Ilios acknowledged. The fact that not once since he had taken her to bed had Lizzie made any reference to what had happened. Not so much as by a look, never mind a word. Because she regretted what had happened? Because her sexual desire for him, once satisfied, had vanished? Either of those alternatives should have been welcomed by him, and yet here he was feeling they were unsatisfactory—that the situation between them was unsatisfactory. It left him feeling that there was unfinished business between them, that he wanted...

He wanted what? To take her back to bed and repeat his reckless behaviour? Double the chances of her becoming pregnant? Was that really what he wanted? The ferocity with which his heart slammed into his ribs caught him off guard. It was the realisation of what could happen that had caused that surge of emotion inside him, that was all. Nothing else. The last thing he wanted was for Lizzie to be carrying his child.

Ilios forced himself to focus on Lizzie's question.

'Yes and no,' he answered. 'It is both similar and different—you will have to judge for yourself. However, what I can tell you is that structurally my ancestor followed Palladio's measurement ratio for the interior, just as he did for the exterior, so the villa follows Palladio's beliefs in the importance of architectural harmony. Internally, the living space forms a classical central square core, within which are six rooms that size-wise form repetitions of one of Palladio's standard modules. For instance, either side of the entrance hall are two rooms which are sixteen Trevisan feet in width by twenty-seven Trevisan feet in length.' He paused, in case what he was saying was going over Lizzie's head, but he could see from her expression that she was following what he was saying perfectly.

'To create a ratio of six to ten,' she agreed. 'The perfect numbers in Renaissance architecture. I've read references to Palladio's buildings being like frozen music, because he adopted the proportions that Pythagoras said produced combinations of notes that fall harmoniously on the human ear.'

Ilios gave an approving nod of his head. 'That Greek connection had great appeal for my ancestor, according to our family lore. As far as Villa Manos goes, in between the smaller rooms—the two I've already mentioned—facing east and the west of the villa, are four more rooms which together have the same Palladio measurements. The central grand salon comprises two of those modules side by side, and the floor plan of the piano nobile is repeated in a second piano nobile over it, with mezzanine rooms in between.'

'Like Villa Cornaro?'

'You're obviously a Palladio fan.'

'It's impossible not to be if you love classical architecture.' Lizzie smiled. 'I was half toying with the idea of training as an architect when my parents died. It hadn't been my first choice of career, but working as an interior designer showed me how important structure is. From there… What is it?' she asked, when she saw how his own expression had changed and hardened.

Reluctantly he told her, 'My father was an architect, and as a boy it was my ambition to follow in his footsteps in that regard—to build modern structures in celebration of Palladio's own style, based on his principles. Of course there wasn't the money, although as a boy I didn't realise that. The Junta imposed such heavy taxes and fines on those who antagonised them, as my grandfather did, that they beggared him. He was left with nothing, and he had to watch Villa Manos falling into disrepair, unable to do anything to halt that process. Keeping it in defiance of the Junta was something of a pyrrhic victory for him. By the time the Junta was deposed there was nothing left for him to sell or mortgage, and certainly no money to educate me to the standard necessary for me to train as an architect. He loved the villa more than he loved any living person.'

Abruptly Ilios stopped speaking, wondering why he had allowed himself to reveal so much about his childhood and his family, telling Lizzie things he have never disclosed before to anyone, much less a woman who had shared his bed.

What was it about her that caused him to react in the way he did? As though she was different—and special? He must not exaggerate the situation, or his own reactions to it, Ilios cautioned himself. It was the fact that Lizzie was knowledgeable about Palladio and his work that had led to him confiding in her the way he had, nothing more.

Lizzie fought back the emotional tears stinging the backs of her eyes as Ilios finished speaking.

'But he must have loved you as well. After all, he left you the villa,' she told him impulsively, wanting instinctively to ease what she knew must be his hurt. Who would *not* be hurt in such circumstances?

'No, my value to him lay in my genes, that is all,' was Ilios's harsh response.

Lizzie ached with sadness for him. Was his own childhood the cause of Ilios's determination not to marry and not to allow any woman to knowingly have his children? Had having to be so self-reliant, unable to trust the one adult he should have been able to turn to, left him so badly scarred that he was unable to trust other human beings himself? It would have taken great emotional strength and endurance and great maturity to have survived the childhood Ilios had had and emerge unscathed from it, far more than any young child could have been expected to have.

Lizzie felt desperately sorry for the little boy Ilios must have been—so sorry, in fact, that she wanted to gather that child up in her arms and hold him safe, give him the same loving childhood she herself had known. But of course that child no longer existed, and the man he had become would scorn her emotions as mere sentiment, she suspected.

'The past is over. Looking back toward it serves no purpose,' Ilios told her curtly. 'We live in the present, after all.'

'That's true, but sometimes we need to look back to what we were to understand what we are now.'

'That is self-indulgence and it also serves no purpose,' Ilios insisted grimly, looking at his watch and adding, 'If you are ready to leave…?'

Lizzie nodded her head. The subject of his childhood and the effect it must have had on him was obviously closed, and she suspected it would remain that way.

It would soon be spring, and the temperature was beginning to rise a little. Wild flowers bloomed by the roadside, the way they had their faces turned up to the sun making Lizzie smile as Ilios drove them towards the east and the peninsula where Villas Manos stood.

Since Ilios was a good driver there was no logical reason for her to feel on edge. No logical reason, perhaps, but since when have the emotions of a woman in love been logical? Lizzie asked herself wryly.

They passed the turn-off for Halkidiki and the famous

Mount Athos peninsula, with its monasteries and its rule that no female was allowed to set foot there, including female animals, and then had stopped briefly at a small tavern for a simple lunch of Greek salad and fruit. It was eaten mainly in the same silence which had pervaded since they had set out.

If Ilios was regretting inviting her to join him, then she was certainly regretting accepting his invitation. She felt rejected and unwanted, deliberately distanced from Ilios by his silence—a silence that her own pride would not allow her to break.

Ilios drove straight to the villa on the western side of the promontory, ignoring the fork in the road to the east where the apartment block had been.

It seemed a lifetime since she had first met Ilios there. Then she had been a single woman, her only concern for her financial situation and the future of her family. Her own emotions as a woman simply had not come into the equation. Now she was married and a wife—at least in the eyes of the world. Her family were financially secure, and her anxiety was all for her own emotions.

Ruby had sent her a photograph of the twins via her mobile, so that Lizzie could see the new school uniforms she had bought for them at Lizzie's insistence that she must do so and that they could afford it. A tender, amused smile curled Lizzie's mouth. The two five-year-olds had looked so proud in their grey flannel trousers and maroon blazers, their dark hair cut short and brushed neatly.

Lizzie loved her nephews. She had been present at their birth, anxious for her young sister, and grieving for the fact that Ruby was having to go through her pain without their parents and without the man who had fathered her children. But when the twins had been born and she had held them all the sad aspects of their birth had been forgotten in the rush of love and joy she had felt.

They had reached the villa now, and even though she had seen it before, and knew what to expect, Lizzie was still filled with admiration and awe as she gazed at its perfect proportions, outlined against the bright blue sky.

The warm cream colour of the villa toned perfectly with the aged darker colour of the marble columns supporting the front portico and with the soft grey-white of the shutters at the windows. The gravel on which the car was resting exactly matched the colour of the marble columns, and the green of the lawns highlighted the darker green of the Cyprus trees lining the straight driveway. The whole scene in front of them was one of visual harmony.

There was no other car parked outside—which Lizzie presumed meant that the man Ilios had come here to see had not as yet arrived.

'We're earlier than I expected, so I'll show you the inside before Andreas arrives,' Ilios announced as he opened the car door for Lizzie and waited for her to get out.

They walked to the entrance side by side. Side by side but feet apart, Lizzie thought sadly as she waited for Ilios to unlock the magnificent double doors.

Above them, where in Italy there would have been the family arms and motto, was an image of a small sailing ship.

'Alexandros Manos earned his fortune as a maritime trader,' Ilios informed her, following her gaze. 'It was his fleet that paid for this land and for the villa.'

Ilios had opened the door, and was stepping back so that Lizzie could precede him inside the villa.

The first thing she noticed was the smell of fresh paint,

unmistakable and instantly recognizable. Her educated nose told her that the smell came from a traditional lime-based paint rather than a modern one.

With the shutters closed the interior was in darkness—until Ilios switched on the lights, causing Lizzie to gasp in astonished delight as she spun round, studying the frescoes that ran the whole way round the double-height central room.

She had seen frescoes before, of course, many of them. But none quite like these.

'Are they scenes from the *Odyssey*?' she asked Ilios uncertainly after she had studied them.

'Yes,' Ilios confirmed. 'Only Odysseus bears a striking resemblance to Alexandros Manos. To have oneself depicted as the hero of the *Odyssey* was, of course, a conceit not uncommon at the time. I've had the frescoes repainted because of the damage they've suffered over the centuries. Luckily we had some sketches of the original scenes to work with. The work still isn't finished yet,' Ilios added, indicating the final panel of the fresco, where a woman was bending over a loom, unpicking a thread, with the outline of a large dog at her feet.

The fresco was badly damaged, with paint peeling from it and marks across it that looked as though someone had scored the panel angrily with something sharp. Even so it was still possible to see what the panel was meant to represent.

'Penelope? The faithful wife?' Lizzie guessed, remembering the legend of how Odysseus's wife Penelope had held off the suitors who wanted to marry her and take possession of Odysseus's kingdom by saying she would only accept one of them when she had finished her tapestry, and then unpicking it every night in secret so that it would never be finished, so sure had she been that her husband would eventually return.

Ilios's terse, 'Yes', told Lizzie that he didn't want to discuss the subject of the panel, so she turned instead to follow him into one of the smaller rooms.

Here scaffolding showed where craftsmen were obviously working to repair the ornate plasterwork ceiling, which Lizzie could see held a central fresco of a family group.

'I had to go to Florence to find the craftspeople to do this work,' Ilios told Lizzie.

'It's a highly skilled job,' Lizzie agreed.

Two hours later Ilios had given her a full tour of the house. The man he was supposed to be meeting had telephoned to say that he would have to cancel and make another appointment. He was unavoidably delayed because his wife had gone into premature labour.

'I hope she and the baby will be all right,' had been Lizzie's immediate and instinctive comment as they'd walked down the return staircase.

The villa would be stunningly beautiful when the restoration work had been completed—a true work of art, in fact. But Lizzie simply could not visualise it as a home.

'It won't be easy, bringing up your sons here,' she felt bound to say.

'I don't plan to live here,' Ilios told her.

Lizzie looked uncertainly at him. 'But I thought—that is, you said that the house had to stay within the family.'

'It does, and it will. But not as a family home. I've got other plans for it. There's a shortage of opportunities for young apprentices to learn the skills that go into maintaining a house like this. I found that out for myself. So I've decided that Villa Manos will become a place where those who want to master those skills can come to learn them. Instead of turning the villa into a dead museum, I plan to turn it into a living workshop—where courses are run for master craftsmen, taught by those who have already mastered those trades themselves.'

'What a wonderful idea.' Lizzie didn't make any attempt to conceal her approval.

'I shall build a house for myself on the other side of the promontory.'

'Where the apartments were?'

'Yes. There will also be an accommodation block, and schoolrooms and proper workshops for the students. They will be situated in the wooded area between the villa and the other side of the promontory—' He broke off as Lizzie's mobile suddenly started to bleep.

'I'm sorry,' she apologised, scrambling in her bag for it so that she could silence it. Her face suddenly broke into a smile as she looked at the image which had flashed up on her screen.

'It's the twins—my nephews,' she told Ilios. 'My sister sent me a photograph of them earlier, in their new school uniforms, and now she's sent me another picture of them.' Lizzie held up the phone so that he could see.

Ilios glanced dismissively at the screen, and then found that he couldn't look away. The young woman in the photograph, kneeling down and clasping a uniform-clad boy in each arm, had that same look of love and happiness on her face as Lizzie herself wore when she was talking about her family. There was no doubting the closeness her family shared, and no doubting Lizzie's love for her sisters and these two small dark-haired boys. Fatherless they might be, but they were laughing into the camera, confident in the love that surrounded them. Neither was there any doubt

about Lizzie's determination to protect her family and
provide for them. If Lizzie herself were to have a child then
she would love it with the same absolute loyalty and
devotion he could see on her face now. A child…his
child… Absorbed in the enormity of what he was thinking,
Ilios didn't notice Lizzie move towards him until he felt
her hand on his arm as she told him, 'It's thanks to you that
they were able to have those uniforms.'

Thanks to him? Ilios tensed against what was happening to him—against the savage dagger-thrusts of pain that
tore into him with Lizzie's words. Because they reminded
him of the truth. The only reason she was here with him
was because he had blackmailed her into marrying him.

He shrugged off Lizzie's hand on his arm, stepping
back from her as he told her, 'There are some interesting
features in the garden. I'll show you.'

Feeling rebuffed, Lizzie switched off her mobile and
returned it to her handbag. Ilios obviously wanted to make
it plain that their relationship was strictly business. He
didn't want to be forced to look at photographs of her
family.

'How long do you think it will be before your cousin
accepts that he doesn't have any grounds to try and overset
your grandfather's will?' she asked Ilios as they headed for
the garden at the rear of the villa.

Here, beyond a wide flagged terrace, steps led down to
what must once have been intricately formal beds of
clipped box, surrounding a pool with a fountain. But Lizzie
wasn't really concentrating on her surroundings. Instead
she was hoping desperately for a miracle—for that miracle
to be Ilios telling her that he had changed his mind about
ending their marriage because he wanted them to be
together for ever.

He shrugged dismissively. 'You are, of course, impatient to return to your family?'

'I do miss them,' Lizzie agreed, her heart sinking. That wasn't the response she had hoped for at all. It was true that she did miss her family, but she was also finding it increasingly difficult to behave as though nothing had happened between her and Ilios. Take now, for instance. When they had come out of the house she had almost put her arm through Ilios's, just as if they were actually a genuine couple. Of course it was because she craved the intimacy of physical closeness with him, just as any woman in love would.

'Regrettably, my lawyers feel that we should remain married for the time being, as a divorce so soon after our wedding would look suspicious. However, you can rest assured that I am every bit as eager to bring our marriage to an end as you,' Ilios announced coldly, his response driven by pride and the need to defend himself from the alien emotions that were threatening him.

The cold words struck into her heart like ice picks. But it was her own fault if she had been hurt, Lizzie told herself resolutely.

'This is what I wanted to show you,' Ilios told her nearly half an hour later, when they had walked through the extensive gardens to the villa and emerged at the side of a pretty man-made lake. He gestured towards a grotto dotted with statuary and ornamented with a small fresh water spring.

'What is it?' Lizzie asked him.

'It's a nymphaeum,' Ilios explained. 'An artificially created grotto for which the statuary has been specifically designed. Villa Barbaro has one—some of its statuary executed by Marcantonio Barbaro, supposedly. It's a conceit, really. A way for the villa-owner to show off either his own talent as a sculptor or that of an artist to whom he was a patron. The lake here needs dredging, and the small temple on the island renovating.'

'The whole place is stunning,' Lizzie told him truthfully. 'I can understand why your ancestor wanted it kept in the family. I do think, though, that your plan to turn it into a living workshop is a wonderful idea—and so very generous. A wonderful gift to future generations, enabling such special skills to be carried on.'

'I'm not motivated by generosity. I've been held up on too many contracts by the lack of skilled artisans—that's why I'm doing it.' Ilios's voice was clipped, as though her praise had annoyed him.

Because he didn't want it? Just as he didn't want her? She mustn't dwell on what she could not have, but instead hold in her heart what they had briefly shared, Lizzie told herself. She mustn't let that joy be overshadowed or diminished.

Nor must she allow the fact that Ilios did not return her feelings to prevent her from behaving as she would have done had she not loved him.

'I've really enjoyed today. Thank you for bringing me and showing me the villa,' she told him, with that in mind, as they headed back to the car for the return journey to Thessaloniki.

He had enjoyed it too, Ilios acknowledged. When he had not been battling with the emotions his conflicting feelings towards her aroused.

On the way back to Thessaloniki they stopped at the same tavern where they had had lunch. The small village overlooked the sea, and the front of the tavern was protected enough from the breeze for it to be warm enough to sit outside.

They'd eaten plump juicy black olives and delicious grilled kebabs, and were just finishing their coffee when it happened. A dull noise like thunder, and the movement of the ground beneath their feet.

The trestle table shifted, spilling Lizzie's coffee, and then Ilios got up, coming towards her and taking hold of her, pushing her down to the ground, covering her with his own body as he warned her, 'It's an earthquake.'

'An earthquake?' she echoed.

'This area's notorious for them. It will be all right—just keep still.'

She had no other option other than to keep still with Ilios's body a protective weight over hers, pinning her to the ground. His hand was cupping the back of her head protectively, pushing her face into his shoulder, allowing her to breathe in the now familiar scent of him. Lizzie just hoped he would assume that the heavy sledgehammer thuds of her heartbeat were caused by her shock and fear of the earthquake rather than by the proximity of their bodies. How fate must be enjoying its joke at her expense, knowing that when she had longed to be held in Ilios's arms these were not the circumstances in which she had envisaged it happening. To be held by him in an embrace outwardly that of the most intimate and tender of lovers which in reality was nothing more than a means of safety felt painfully ironic, even if his prompt actions were for her own benefit.

'What's that?' she asked anxiously above the growing noise she could hear.

'Just a few stones and boulders dislodged by the quake rolling down the hillside.'

Lizzie gasped as the earth moved again, in a shudder she could feel right through her body, causing Ilios to tighten his hold on her. Had he loved her, this moment would have been filled with the most intense emotion—and surely would ultimately have resulted in them celebrating their survival and their love for one another in the most intimate way possible once they had had the privacy to do so. Sex was, after all, the only human activity that combined life, birth and even a small taste of death in that moment when it felt as though one flew free into infinity.

Ilios. Why had she had to fall in love with him? Why couldn't she have simply wanted him on a physical level and nothing more? Because she was a woman, and the female sex, no matter how much it might wish for things to be different, was genetically geared to making an emotional commitment?

The earth had steadied, and so had her heartbeat, slowing to match the sturdy tempo of Ilios's. In a situation that would normally have filled her with fear for her own safety she had felt completely secure, protected—safe because of him. But here in Ilios's arms there was no emotional safety for her, only emotional danger, Lizzie reminded herself.

Against her ear Ilios spoke again. 'That should be it now, but we'd better stay where we are for a few more minutes.'

The warmth of his breath sent small shudders of sensual delight rippling over her nerve-endings, and the knowledge that his lips were so close to her flesh made her want to compel them even closer. Memories of how it had felt to have him caressing her skin with the stroke of his tongue-tip broke through the embargo she had placed on them.

'Will it affect the villa?' Lizzie asked, genuinely concerned about the villa but equally intent on distracting herself from thinking so intimately about Ilios and how much she loved him.

'No. The promontory isn't affected by the fault line.'

Lizzie could hear voices as people called out to one another. Ilios lifted his body from hers. She badly wanted to beg him not to do so—and not because of the earthquake. He stood up, and then reached down to help her to her feet.

'You've got dust on your face.'

Before she could stop him he leaned towards her, brushing her cheek with his hand.

She wanted to stay like this for ever, Lizzie thought achingly. With Ilios's hand on her skin, his gaze on hers, his arm supporting her—just as though she genuinely did matter to him, just as though he cared about her and wanted to protect her because he loved her. She moved towards him yearningly, only to have him move back.

What was happening to him? Ilios asked himself grimly. Increasingly his own behaviour was so alien to what he knew of himself that witnessing it was like confronting a stranger wearing his skin. A stranger who was challenging him for full possession of himself? A stranger who owed his existence to the arrival of Lizzie Wareham in his life? A stranger whose first thought was to protect Lizzie? Why?

Because it was in his own interests to protect her. He had a vested interest in her safety after all.

No one in the village seemed particularly disturbed by the tremor. Everyone was going about their normal business, and men were working to clear the debris from the hillside from the road as Lizzie got to her feet.

'Are you okay?' Ilios asked her.

'Yes, thanks to you.'

Oh, yes, he was definitely withdrawing from her—rejecting her gratitude, rejecting anything remotely emotional between them, and of course rejecting her physically.

Ilios stepped back from her physically as well as emotionally with a brisk nod of his head. 'In ancient times they used to believe that it was the gods' anger that was responsible for these tremors,' he commented a few minutes later as he opened the car door for Lizzie. 'Now we construct buildings especially designed to cope with the movement caused by them.'

CHAPTER THIRTEEN

RIDICULOUSLY, since she had done next to nothing all day other than sightsee and enjoy the rooftop garden of Ilios's apartment, Lizzie felt incredibly tired. She tried to stifle a yawn and look instead as though she was enjoying the reception she and Ilios were attending as part of an incentive by the Greek government to attract new business to the area. Naturally Ilios, as head of a locally based business which was successful internationally, was in great demand, and he had apologised for having to desert her to talk business with someone who had asked to be introduced to him.

She wasn't the only wife left to stand alone nursing a drink, Lizzie recognised as she glanced round the elegant hotel ballroom where the reception was being held. But her glass merely contained water. Champagne was something she was determined to avoid for as long as she was married to Ilios.

A smile of recognition from one of the women she had met at the gallery opening had her heading towards her in relief. Now that she was a little wiser about Thessaloniki society she dressed accordingly—overdressed, in fact, by her normal standards. Tonight, in addition to her designer dress in yellow silk, she was also wearing the jewellery. Ilios had a position to maintain, after all, and not just for the sake of his own personal status. The employees of Manos Construction depended on him, and on the success of the business. An immaculately coiffed and groomed wife said that a man had both good taste and money—reassuring values where other businessmen were concerned, no matter how much Lizzie might wish for a simpler and more straightforward way of doing business.

Engrossed in her own thoughts as she wove her way through the crowded room, she didn't see Ilios's cousin—to whom she had been introduced by Ilios earlier—making a beeline for her, until he was standing in front of her blocking her way.

Lizzie's heart sank.

When Ilios had warned her that his cousin was likely to be present she had been curious to meet him. Her private view was that Ilios, for perfectly good reasons rooted in their shared childhood, had turned him into a more unpleasant figure than he actually was.

It had taken less than a minute in Tino Manos's company for her to recognise that she had been wrong. If anything, Ilios's cousin was even more unpleasant than Ilios had said.

'So,' he announced now, with an unpleasant leer, 'an opportunity to talk to the new bride, my cousin-in-law, without Ilios standing over us.'

As he spoke Tino's gaze was fixed on her breasts, discreetly covered by the high neckline of the silk dress which wasn't in the least bit provocative. Nevertheless, the way Ilios's cousin was looking at her made Lizzie feel like crossing her arms over her chest, to protect her body from his unwanted visual inspection.

It was strange how you could sometimes know the

minute you met a person whether or not you were going to like them, Lizzie reflected, and tried not to show how desperately she wanted to escape.

Short and thickset, with overly familiar sharp dark eyes, Tino Manos was the kind of man Lizzie knew she would have disliked no matter who he was related to. She could understand now all too easily why Ilios had spoken as he had when she had suggested that for the sake of his sons he should try to 'mend fences' with his cousin. No sane parent would ever want to entrust his vulnerable children's emotional wellbeing and future to a man like this.

'You are to be congratulated on having caught Ilios. You must have something very special indeed to have persuaded him to give up his freedom having always sworn that he would never marry.'

Lizzie fought hard not to show how offensive she found his unsubtle hints as to why Ilios might have married her and to remain detached. The way Tino was looking at her and the tone of his voice repelled her physically and emotionally, and it was with great relief that she heard Ilios answering his cousin in an even tone.

'Yes, she does, Tino—and that something is my love.'

There was no need for Lizzie to act as she turned to her husband and gave him a speaking look of gratitude for his intervention.

'Love? I thought that was something you'd foresworn.'

Tino was like a dog with its teeth into something it wasn't going to release, Lizzie recognized.

'So did I,' Ilios agreed. 'Until I met Lizzie.'

As he spoke he turned towards her, smiling tenderly down into her eyes, reaching out to take hold of her hand, rubbing his thumb gently over her skin in a gesture that both caressed and reassured.

'And married her with such speed that you didn't even have time to invite anyone to the wedding.'

Tino was suspicious, Lizzie felt sure. Her hand trembled against Ilios's, and the look she gave him mirrored what she was feeling.

'I didn't want to risk losing her,' Ilios responded, still smiling down at her. 'I never want to lose her.'

As he spoke he bent his head and kissed her, his actions taking Lizzie by surprise. She knew that Ilios was putting on an act for his cousin, but still she had not expected this. Beneath his, her own lips softened and clung. Without intending to do so she placed her hand on his arm and moved closer to him, her whole body succumbing to her love for him, yearning toward him. Beneath the silk of her dress she could feel her nipples firming and aching, desire stirring and then quickening in the pit of her stomach. Unable to stop herself, she lifted her hand from his arm to his face, tracing the line of his jaw with achingly longing fingertips.

Ilios lifted his mouth from hers, causing Lizzie to open her eyes and look up at him. Her hand trembled against his skin, betraying her emotions, and her chest lifted with the demand from her lungs for extra oxygen. The words *I want you so much* and *Let's go home* formed inside her head, but had to be denied speech.

'So, how did the two of you meet?'

Tino's voice was an unwanted intrusion, reminding Lizzie of her real role, as a paid-for pretend wife. She compared all the pain that that brought her with the impossible fantasy she longed for. A fantasy in which Ilios really did love, really had meant what he had just said, really had meant the way he had just kissed her…

'Fate brought us together, Tino,' Ilios answered his cousin, continuing, 'Now, if you'll excuse us…?'

Ilios was drawing her away, his hand resting against the hollow of her back as he guided her towards Ariadne Constantin—the woman who had smiled at her earlier.

CHAPTER FOURTEEN

LIZZIE had to wait until she and Ilios were in the car and on their way home, having arranged to have dinner with the Constantins later in the week, to tell him, 'You were right about your cousin. It would be impossible to entrust the future of your sons to him. Do you think he believed what you said about us?'

'I certainly hope so,' Ilios answered.

Because he wanted to get rid of her, of course.

Ilios was annoyed with himself. Lizzie's admission that she had been wrong about his cousin had reminded him of her earlier warnings about the vulnerability of his children should anything happen to him. Why should he be concerned about what she thought? Why should the dangerous thought that Lizzie would be a good mother find its way into his head? He knew he had made the right decision with regard to his own life, and Lizzie could have as many children as she wanted just so long as they weren't his.

'I'll say goodnight,' Lizzie told him at the apartment, as she went to put away her coat. 'After all, I'm sure you have work you want to do.'

Why had she said that? Ilios wasn't stupid—just the opposite, in fact. He was very perceptive, and he was bound to hear the acid note in her voice and guess that she was deliberately needling him. She held her breath, waiting for him to challenge her, but instead he turned away from her, leaving her feeling relieved that her reckless behaviour hadn't provoked any comeback.

In the dressing room of the master bedroom she hung up her coat and warned herself that if he *had* demanded an explanation of her comment, he might easily have worked out that it had been provoked by her longing for him to take her to bed again, for his love.

It was all because of that kiss he had given her earlier in the evening—the way it had made her ache with the pain of her unrequited love for him.

In the living room Ilios opened his laptop. Lizzie was right, he did have work to do—and, as he had discovered many years ago, for him work wasn't just the panacea that stopped all his pain, it was also his most constant and trusted companion, his closest ally in the fight to remain independent of all human emotional demands. It sustained and supported him, and he knew that within seconds of studying the screen in front of him all thoughts of Lizzie Wareham and the unwanted emotions she aroused within him would disappear.

Only they didn't. No matter how hard he focussed on the screen, all he could see was Lizzie's image inside his head.

What was going on? Whatever it was, he didn't want it, Ilios thought savagely. There was no place in his life for it—or for her. But the harder he clung to that thought, to his denial of what he really wanted, the more his body ached for Lizzie. His body. That was all. That was all it was—a physical desire conjured up out of a lack of regular sex and the fact that he was sharing his living space with a woman. Any woman would have had the same effect on him. Any woman? Then why was it *her* image he could see inside his head, *her* body he ached to hold, *her* love for which he now hungered?

No. He categorically refused to accept the thought that had somehow slipped into his head. If he wanted anything from her then it was merely sex. Nothing more.

Prove it, an inner voice challenged him. Go to her now and take her in your arms, hold her and caress her and prove that when you do those things all you feel is a clinical sexual response, without anything emotional to pollute its physical purity.

Ilios looked towards the door. This was ridiculous. He didn't have anything to prove to anyone—least of all himself. But somehow he was on his feet and heading towards the master bedroom.

Lizzie was just getting into bed when the door opened and Ilios strode into the room.

'I thought that tonight I'd have an early night myself,' he told her, before disappearing into the dressing room.

Lying beneath the bedclothes, her stomach quivering with a mixture of uncertainty and excitement, Lizzie tried to breathe normally and relax, warning herself that Ilios probably hadn't meant anything other than exactly what he had said.

There was no need for him to do this, Ilios assured himself, as he stood under the jets of the shower.

Was he afraid that he couldn't prove what he had claimed? that inner voice goaded him.

No! Ilios denied. He stepped out of the shower and reached for a towel. If she hadn't touched his face and looked at him the way she had earlier on this evening, when he'd been forced to put on that display of newly married bliss for Tino, then this wouldn't be happening. He wouldn't be aching the way he was for her now. No? If that was all that had made him ache for her, then what was his excuse for the fact that he had ached for her in the same way every night since that first time?

It was sex—that was all. Sex.

He flung down the towel. There was still time to stop this, still time to walk away and to use his will-power to silence the voice inside him.

There might still be time, but where was the desire? That, Ilios acknowledged as he opened the bedroom door, was all for Lizzie.

She was lying on Ilios's side of the bed. How could she have forgotten?

'I'm on your side of the bed,' she told him as he came towards her. 'I'll move over.'

'Why?' Ilios asked her softly. 'When we're going to be sharing the same space?'

Lizzie felt her heart give a gigantic thump, and then her body filled with an anticipatory pleasure that poured through her like melted honey.

That was nothing compared with what she felt when Ilios got into the bed and drew her close to him. Like her, he was naked, and the feel of his skin against hers was a sensual caress almost beyond bearing.

This shouldn't be happening. Not now, when she knew that she loved him. It had been different before, but now... Now she was deceiving him, taking from him something he would not want to give her. Ilios was touching her, stroking his fingertips down the sensitive flesh of her inner arm and making her shudder openly in responsive pleasure. Lizzie lifted her own hand to his shoulder, intending to tell him they must stop, but somehow the sensation of the warm, firm ball of male sinew and muscle beneath her touch overwhelmed her good intentions, seducing away her will-power to do anything other than give in to her own need.

Closing her eyes, Lizzie shaped the muscles of his back, her own nerve-endings recording the pleasure of each touch. Was male flesh really different from female flesh— thicker, sleeker, more warm, sensual satin than soft silk, somehow intrinsically male in its construction? Or was it merely her own response to knowing that the flesh she was touching belonged to Ilios that made her feel that?

As he kissed her and held her Ilios's desire for her ran like ribbons of fire, until it filled his heart and his veins, spilling out into his touch so that it patterned his feelings for her on her flesh.

Cupped within his hand, the soft weight of her breast fitted as perfectly as though it had been created for his hold alone, and the erotic sensitivity of her nipple as it responded to his caress was responsive in that way only to his touch. The arch of her body inviting the possession of his was aroused only by and for him, as though they had been made for one another and only one another.

How could such a delicate touch have the power to drain from him the resistance of a lifetime? How could it seem to offer sanctuary and comfort? How could it possibly have the power to transform him from a man to whom emotions were the enemy to a man who craved…? A man who craved what?

Ilios moved restlessly against his own thoughts, against his own weakness in allowing himself this unfamiliar need to give the essence of himself into the safekeeping of another. He cupped Lizzie's face so that he could kiss her. Kissing her and feeling her response to him re-established his role as the one in charge of what was happening. And his was the responsibility for them both, Ilios warned himself—a responsibility he had already neglected once.

Beneath Ilios's kiss Lizzie breathed a sigh of delight. It was impossible not to let her hand follow its own inclinations and drift down the lean length of his body, past the flat male curve of his hip, and then come to rest at the base of his spine. The pressure of Ilios's mouth on her own increased, his arms tightening around her as he half rolled her beneath him. Eagerly Lizzie parted her lips, her tongue caressing his, her fingertips stroking the shallow hollow where his spine ended.

Was it her love for Ilios that made the intimacy they were now sharing so heart-achingly intense? Lizzie wondered emotionally. It must be; there could be no other explanation, surely, for the sense of deep intimacy and connection she felt towards him.

She moaned softly with delight as Ilios moved over her, answering the pressure of her growing need. The pleasure from his hands spreading her thighs and his lips tasting her sex took from her both the ability and the will to do anything other than give herself over to him as he moved up her body, his flesh gleaming in the moonlight, erect and taut. Lizzie reached out towards it, encircling the swollen head of his sex, engrossed in the sensation of possessing him.

What had been pleasure had now become a fierce beating urgency—a primeval drive strong enough to crush all obstacles in its way.

How could the pleasure of another's touch be so intense that it invaded every part of him, making his nerve-endings cry out within him under its onslaught? He wanted Lizzie to go on caressing him as she was for ever. He wanted her to stroke and know every bit of him. He wanted— As if a sheer drop had appeared out of nowhere in a misty landscape Ilios's thoughts skidded to a halt as he recognised the danger he was facing. He could not, *would* not allow himself to feel like this. It went against everything he had worked for and planned for. It must not happen. It had to be destroyed.

Abruptly Ilios forced himself to release Lizzie, pulling back from her, leaving her without a backward look or a word of explanation.

Ilios had gone. She was alone in the bed that had so recently been such a wonderful place of intimacy and shared desire but which was now a place of harsh reality and emptiness.

Curled up against her pain, Lizzie tensed her jaw against the agonised cry of despair burning her throat. What had she expected? That the impossible would happen and Ilios would declare his love for her? She was twenty-seven, not seventeen, and surely what had happened to her young sister had shown her the damage that could be done when a woman was foolish enough to believe that her love for a man had the power to change him, somehow conjure from him a reciprocal love for her.

Ilios did not love her. He had made that plain in the way that he had recoiled from her, rejecting her with that look of furious disbelief that had told her more clearly than any words that he not only didn't love her, but he actively wished she was not there.

CHAPTER FIFTEEN

LIZZIE suppressed a small guilty yawn, afraid she might actually fall asleep in her dinner if she wasn't careful.

She was regretting now having agreed that it was a good idea, at the reception a week before, when Ariadne Constantin had suggested that the four or them go for dinner together, to a new restaurant that had recently opened to rave reviews. Especially in view of the distance that Ilios had deliberately created between them. He barely looked at her any more, never mind spoke to her or touched her. There had not been any further invitations to accompany him on site visits during the day, and nor was he discussing any aspect of his life or his plans with her any more. It was, Lizzie acknowledged bleakly, as though he hated her being there and bitterly resented the fact he had had to marry her—even though it had been his own decision.

The food, a Greek take on Australian-Eastern fusion cooking, was delicious, and the light sauces accompanying the fish and meat courses mouthwateringly tempting, but Lizzie had no appetite for them. She was far too unhappy. Was her constant tiredness perhaps a symptom of the misery she was feeling? Was that why she yearned to close her eyes and blot out reality?

Just remembering the curtness in his voice and the way he had turned away from her now was enough to close up her throat and sting the back of her eyes with the embarrassing threat of unwanted tears. Her reaction was surely more that of a hormonal teenager than an adult woman, and certainly not one she could ever remember having before. But then she had never loved Ilios before.

Lizzie watched enviously as Ariadne and her husband got up to dance on the restaurant's small dance floor. It must be heaven to be held so close in the arms of the man you loved in a small and discreet public demonstration of the love between you. Her body trembled in response to the intensity of her emotions.

The Constantins were returning to the table. Stavros Constantin was ordering more wine. Lizzie shook her head when the waiter moved to fill her glass. She hadn't touched alcohol since the night she had drunk champagne and she and Ilios made love—had had sex, she corrected herself fiercely. That was all it had been—sex—lust—that was what she must remember. She certainly wasn't going to risk having a drink now. In her current emotionally vulnerable frame of mind there was no saying what she might attempt to do, or how much she might try to humiliate herself once they were alone together.

The other three drank their wine, then Ariadne got up, asking if, like her, Lizzie wanted to visit the ladies'.

Nodding her head, Lizzie got up too. Anything would be better than having to sit next to Ilios, knowing how eager he was to get rid of her.

Once in the cloakroom, Lizzie felt the tiredness that had threatened to overwhelm her earlier catch up with her again, causing her to smother yet another yawn. She apologised to Ariadne as she did so, hoping that the other woman wouldn't think her rude.

'Don't worry,' Ariadne responded. 'I understand. I was exactly the same when I was first pregnant with our son. I'd been expecting morning sickness, but instead what I got was sleeping sickness.'

Pregnant. The cloakroom spun dizzily round her and Lizzie had to cling to the basin.

Ariadne, obviously concerned, reached out to her.

'I'm all right,' Lizzie reassured her. 'It's just that I hadn't thought—'

She stopped abruptly, but Ariadne had obviously guessed the truth because she put her hand to her lips and then exclaimed, 'Oh! You didn't realise that you might be pregnant—and now I am the first to know and it should have been Ilios. Don't worry—I shan't say a word—not even to Stavros.' She gave Lizzie's arm a comforting little squeeze, and offered, 'If you would like, I could give you the name of my maternity doctor. He is very good.'

'That's kind of you, but...but I don't actually think that I *am* pregnant,' Lizzie fibbed. She was still in shock, battling to accept the reality of the situation, torn between tears of despair and joy. She longed with all her heart to believe that the man she loved would react to the news of the child they had created together with pride and love. But how could that happen when Ilios did not love her?

Pregnant. She was pregnant. It seemed so obvious now that she couldn't believe she had not realised for herself. What should she do? Ilios had a right to know, of course. What would he say? What would he do? He wanted sons. Would the knowledge that she was carrying his child soften his heart towards her or harden it? Lizzie wished she knew.

But if he rejected her and their child then at least his son or daughter would have a family who loved it in England.

A powerful surge of maternal need to protect her unborn child raced through her. Ilios might not want the child they had created together, but she would love it—doubly so, because she would love it for itself and because it came from Ilios.

Back at their table, she wanted to yawn again. On the other side of the table Ariadne smiled knowingly at her, telling her husband, 'Lizzie is tired. She isn't yet used to our habit of eating late, I expect. Ilios, you must take her home and look after her.'

Lizzie stiffened, horrified that despite her promise Ariadne might announce that she thought Lizzie was pregnant. But to her relief Ariadne announced that they too did not want a late night as her mother was babysitting.

They left the restaurant together, and said their goodbyes in a flurry of hugs and kisses in the street next to their parked cars. Ariadne's warm hug for Lizzie was patently meaningful.

Leaning back against the comfortable support of the passenger seat of Ilios's car, whilst he drove them back to the apartment, Lizzie closed her eyes, her thoughts driven by panic and despair. She was pregnant. She was carrying Ilios's child. Despite the turmoil of her thoughts, somewhere deep inside Lizzie there was a small pool of calm and joy in the knowledge that she was carrying the most precious gift that life could give: the child of the man she loved.

CHAPTER SIXTEEN

LIZZIE gave Maria a wan smile as they stepped into the lift
together. It was a week since she had realised that she was
pregnant, and she still hadn't told Ilios. But then she hadn't
really had much opportunity to do so, since he avoided her
as much as he could. Lizzie wished that she was braver—
that she had the courage to confront him, to tell him outright
that he could treat her as he chose but his child had a right
to his love. She had been out for a walk to try and clear her
thoughts. Ilios was being so cold to her that she knew it was
pointless her hoping that he would ever return her love.

The lift moved silently upwards. Lost in the despair of
her own thoughts, Lizzie forgot to keep her back turned
away from the glass wall and the yawning cavity below,
the sight of which always made her feel nervous. She had
suffered from a fear of heights for as long as she could
remember, and the movement of the lift and its glass structure only made her feel worse.

A wave of dizziness engulfed her, making her lose her
balance. The lift had stopped, but she felt too nauseous to
move.

Maria took control, taking hold of her arm and supporting her as she guided her determinedly from the lift, across

the hallway into the apartment. Lizzie felt too unwell to do anything but allow Maria to do so. A cold sweat had broken out on her forehead and her stomach was churning. When Maria released her to close the door, Lizzie slid to the floor in a dead faint.

When she came round Maria was kneeling on the floor beside her, her face flushed with excited delight as she a patted Lizzie's hand maternally and assured her, 'You do not worry. It is just the baby Ilios make with you makes you faint. He will be a big fine boy. Already he is causing his mama trouble. You stay there. I telephone Ilios and tell him to get doctor to come.'

'No!' Lizzie protested, horrified. 'No, Maria, please…' she begged her. This wasn't how she wanted Ilios to learn that he was to become a father. 'There's no need. I'm perfectly all right.' But it was no use. Maria already had the phone in her hand and was speaking at speed into it in Greek, gesturing as she did so.

Very carefully Lizzie got to her feet and made her way to the living room, where she sat down on one of the sofas. She still felt queasy, and slightly dizzy, but then she hadn't eaten any breakfast this morning. She'd planned to eat something whilst she was out, but she hadn't, and now she suspected the baby was making its displeasure known. A haunted smile touched her mouth as Lizzie remembered how firm she had been with Ruby about eating properly when she had been carrying the twins.

She could hear Ilios's voice in the hallway now, as he spoke in Greek to Maria. Her heart was jumping, her mouth dry. Matters had been taken out of her hands and there was no going back. Thanks to Maria, Ilios would now know that he was going to be a father. What would he say? What would he do?

The door opened and he came into the living room, striding towards her and then standing over her. He wasn't wearing a jacket, and his shirt emphasised the powerful width of his shoulders—shoulders that a woman could lean on, so long as that woman wasn't her.

'Maria says you fainted.'

Ilios's voice was harsh—with anger? Lizzie fought down the threatened return of her earlier nausea. Ginger biscuits—that was what she needed. They had worked for Ruby, she remembered.

'Is it true that there is to be a child?' Ilios demanded grimly.

Lizzie couldn't bring herself to speak. She could only nod her head, well able to imagine how unwelcome to him her confirmation would be.

Anger seized Ilios—a furious, savage, blinding rage that exploded inside him like a fireball, devouring reason, humanity and compassion. This was the very last thing he wanted—to be tied to anyone. And especially to this woman, who he had been fighting to keep out of his thoughts, his desires and his emotions, by anything, but most of all by a child. A living, breathing human life that would bind the three of them together with cords that no mere man had the power to break. Ilios wanted to bunch his fists and cry out to the gods his denial of this claim on him. He did not want it and never would.

'You did this deliberately—despite the fact that you knew I would not want it,' he accused Lizzie, conveniently forgetting that he himself had played the greater role in his child's conception. 'No doubt you were hoping to force me into accepting both you and your child—a child I expect you see as a meal ticket that will enable you to live in comfort for the rest of your life.'

Lizzie felt sick with grief and pain.

'No!' she told him. 'That is not what I thought.'

'No?' Ilios challenged her. 'Do you think I am such a fool that I can't see now what you *really* wanted when you claimed to desire me? What you really desired was what you are now carrying within you. My child—born into a legal marriage. A child that I cannot deny or refuse to accept. A child that will have a lifelong financial claim on me.'

'That's not true,' Lizzie denied frantically.

'You had it all planned, didn't you?' Ilios gave her a look of biting contempt. 'Well, I refute your claim and I refute your child. Both you and it are as nothing to me. Less than nothing.'

That was all Lizzie needed to hear. Ilios's cruel words had fallen on her like blows—blows she would not allow her child to bear.

She stood up, despite the fact that she felt so weak, and started to walk towards the door.

When she reached it she turned round and told Ilios proudly, 'Your child might be less than nothing to you, Ilios, but to me he or she is the most precious thing in my life. You're right. I *did* hope for lifelong security from you when I told you I desired you, even if at the time I didn't recognise it for what it was myself. But the lifelong security I wanted wasn't your money, it was your love— in exchange for my love for you. Now that you've made it plain that that can never be, I shall remove both my unwanted presence and your equally unwanted child from your life—permanently.'

'Good,' Ilios told her coldly. 'And the sooner the better.'

CHAPTER SEVENTEEN

ILIOS had gone out. Lizzie didn't know where. She wasn't going to cry. What would be the point? Instead she did everything that had to be done. She booked herself a seat on the first available flight, packed her trolley case. She wasn't going to take anything that had come to her via Ilios—except, of course, his child. But then he didn't want that child—had denied it, spoken callously and dismissively of it.

She was crying after all. Tears were flooding her eyes to run down her face before she could stop them. Carefully she wiped them away with a tissue.

She had done everything she needed to do, including calling herself a cab.

The intercom rang.

It was time for her to go.

She dropped the tissue beside the notepad next to the telephone, where she had written down her flight number, and headed for the door.

Would she have gone yet? Ilios hoped so, he told himself as he unlocked the door to his apartment and went inside.

But it wasn't pleasure or even relief that gripped him

and twisted his emotions with ruthless, painful intensity when he stood in the master bedroom. Only the lingering echo of Lizzie's scent remained to show that she had ever been there. On the bedside table on his side of the bed were her engagement and wedding rings. He picked them up. Lizzie had such slender fingers, elegant hands. The rings felt warm. Ilios curled his hand round them. Lizzie's warmth. An image slid into his head of Lizzie's hands holding their child, Lizzie's face looking down at it, her eyes warm with love.

Fresh anger filled him. Broodingly he pushed the rings into his pocket. What was the matter with him? He was behaving like…like a lovesick fool. He was the one who had wanted her to go. Who had forced her to go. Forced her to go even when he had seen how unwell she looked. What if she fainted again? What if she did? Why should he care?

Ilios walked into the dressing room and removed his jacket. A wisp of lace trapped in the closed doors of Lizzie's closet caught his eye. She'd obviously missed something when she'd packed. He pulled open the door, a fresh surge of anger burning through him when he saw all the clothes hanging there. The clothes he had bought her. What was she trying to prove? Did she really think he'd be impressed because she'd left them? Well, he wasn't. The truth was that he would far rather she had taken them with her. Why? Because he was afraid that they would remind him of her, and that he might start regretting what he had done?

Of course not. That was rubbish. Was it? Wasn't he already missing her? Hadn't he regretted his cruelty to her almost from the minute he had left the apartment?

Didn't the fact that he was here now, pacing the floor,

unable to work, unable to stop thinking about her, tell him anything about his own feelings? About her—Lizzie?

Lizzie.

Ilios sat down heavily in the chair next to the telephone, dropping his head into his hands in defeat.

Alone in the silent space which, despite all his attempts to stop it from being so, was filled with intangible memories of Lizzie's presence within it, Ilios glanced at the telephone. His body stiffened as he saw the piece of paper on which Lizzie had written her flight number and its time of departure. Another hour and she would be gone out of his life. There was a tissue beside the telephone marked with mascara—had she cried? Because of him? The sudden ring of the telephone filled him with a surge of fierce hope. Lizzie. It had to be.

He snatched up the receiver, his heart pounding as he demanded, 'Lizzie?' only to be flooded with disappointment when he realised that his caller was merely an acquaintance.

After he had got rid of him Ilios replaced the receiver and stood motionless, staring into space, whilst his heart thudded with sledgehammer blows that were pounding, beating into him the message, the knowledge that he had fought so hard to deny.

Pain wrenched through him, tearing at his heart, clawing at it, filling him with despair.

He loved Lizzie. He loved her and he had lost her.

Nothing was the same in his life because nothing could *be* the same. The anger he felt, the fury, the grim determination to destroy what had taken root in his heart, belonged not to a brave man but to a coward. It wasn't his love for Lizzie that was threatening his future, but his attempts to destroy it. As though light had replaced darkness Ilios could see now, when it was too late, how empty his life had been—and would be without her. In the short time they had been together she had changed him so completely, in so many different ways, that he felt he was still getting to know the person he now was—and he was in need of her support to help him do so. She had taught him so much, but there was still much he had to learn. How could he teach the sons who would follow him to be the men Ilios now knew he wanted them to be on his own? He couldn't. Those sons, just like him, needed Lizzie. They all needed her love.

When he thought of the sons he had planned to have, and the manner in which he had planned their conception, inside his head he saw them living in the shadows, deprived of the happiness they would have known had Lizzie been their mother. He wanted to stop time and turn it back, to that moment when he had still been holding her in his arms. He could have listened to what his own heart had been trying to tell him instead of resolutely denying it. Could have told her that he was nothing without her, and could have begged her to love him. Now it was too late.

Too late. Inside his head Ilios had an image of himself as a small child, standing on the quayside with Tino and his grandfather whilst he watched his mother and her new husband stepping onto his sailing boat. His mother had held out her arms to him, telling him to jump into them. He had desperately wanted to go to her, he remembered, but he had known that his grandfather disapproved of her remarrying.

'Mummy's boy, mummy's boy,' Tino had taunted him, and so he had hesitated, and then had had to watch his mother's smile disappear to be replaced by coldness as she turned away from him.

That had been the last time he had seen her. A month later she had drowned.

If he had jumped, if he had taken that risk, if he had trusted her love to keep him safe, how different would his life have been?

Too late.

Ilios reached for his mobile. For the man with courage there was no such thing as too late. There was merely further to travel to reach what he most wanted.

CHAPTER EIGHTEEN

Her flight had been called, but Lizzie had been attacked by a sudden surge of nausea that had forced her to make a dash for the ladies', where she now still was as she prayed for the threatening sickness to subside.

She hadn't texted her sisters yet. She was still trying to work out what to tell them. Another surge of nausea engulfed her.

Ilios was out of the helicopter as soon as it landed, ducking low to avoid the draught from its still-turning props as he ran across the tarmac and into the terminal building. He'd been lucky that the helicopter service he used had had a pilot on standby.

The gate for Lizzie's flight had closed, but Ilios wasn't going to let a little thing like that stop him. He'd hire a private jet and follow her all the way back to Manchester if he had to.

'Last call for Flight E20 for Manchester. Will passenger Elizabeth Wareham please report to Gate 10…'

Lizzie hadn't boarded? Ilios looked round the empty waiting area. Then where was she?

* * *

Lizzie grabbed her handbag and hurried out of the ladies'. Her sickness had finally subsided, but if she didn't hurry she was going to miss her flight.

They were calling her name again. Her old name, which she had realized with shock was still the name on her passport—the name to which she was now returning. It had only seemed a few yards when she had rushed down to the ladies', but now it seemed miles. There was the gate—and Ilios was standing beside it.

Lizzie came to an abrupt halt.

'I need to talk to you,' Ilios told her

'I'll miss my flight.'

Taking a deep breath, Ilios held out his hand to her.

'Please Lizzie.'

She wanted to refuse. She should refuse—for the sake of her baby if not for herself—but somehow she couldn't.

Ilios was taking advantage of her hesitation, telling the girl that she wouldn't be flying and assuring her that since she only had hand luggage there was no need for the flight to be delayed whilst her cases were unloaded.

'Let's go and sit down,' Ilios suggested. 'You shouldn't be standing so much, not when…'

He was expressing concern for them? For her and the baby?

That made her feel so shaky that she needed to sit down, Lizzie admitted, as she let him guide her to a chair and then sit down next to her.

'I was wrong to say what I did. Very wrong,' Ilios told her. 'I want you to stay. The fact that you are to have my child changes everything. Its place is here in Greece with me, and yours with it. You are both my responsibility. It is my duty to provide for you.' How stiff and cumbersome the words sounded, but he didn't know any other way to say what he wanted to say.

'Duty is no substitute for love, Ilios,' Lizzie told him. 'And I can't live in a marriage without love. Wanting something you can't have is corrosive. It embitters and destroys. Being trapped in a marriage that isn't wanted drives the one who doesn't love to crave their freedom, and from that contempt and hostility will grow. I don't want our child to grow up in that kind of environment, torn between two parents who are together only because of it. It is too much of a burden to place on a child. It's better that I leave.' She paused. 'Please don't make this harder for me than it already is. I'll tell him or her all about you—how special you are, how proud it can be to be your child and to have you as its father.'

She had to stop because of the emotion choking her throat. She wanted badly to touch him, to trace the shape of his face and give him her love—the love she knew he did not want.

'I'll tell it that you wanted us to be with you, and that it is my fault we aren't. And when I do I'll tell it too how much I love you, and how I couldn't bear to burden you with that love when I knew you didn't want it and hadn't asked for it. I can't promise, though, to tell it that its mother was foolish enough to mistake love for lust. I hope you will be happy, Ilios, and that life will send you someone you can truly love, because…'

'It already has—only I was too afraid to accept it, Lizzie.' He caught hold of her arm, his voice hoarse with desperation. 'I love you. Please give me a second chance. We belong together—you and me and our child.'

Lizzie shook her head. 'You're just saying that because of the baby. Because you think you have to. Because—'

Ilios stopped her. 'I'm saying it because it's the truth.'

One look at her face told him that no matter how hard he tried to convince her she was not going to believe him.

He took a deep breath.

'Lizzie, do you know why this—' he touched her still flat stomach '—happened?'

'Of course. It happened because I desired you.'

Ilios shook his head.

'No, it happened because I allowed it to happen—because secretly I wanted it to happen, even if I wouldn't let myself recognise that fact at the time. Something in me, something stronger and braver than I was, knew what I most needed.'

He was holding her hand in his own, making her feel safe and protected, making her wish…

'I admire you more than I believed it possible to admire anyone—man or woman. I respect you and I value you—as a person, not just as the woman I love. Before I knew I loved you I knew that I wanted you to be the mother of my sons. I knew that the night we made love. I knew it, and because I knew it I deliberately chose to ignore the fact that we weren't using any contraception. Even if I refused to recognise it at the time I know now that I wanted you to have my child, Lizzie. I wanted to tie you to me and I knew that you could not have a child and not love it. Please stay. Please stay and let me prove to you that I do love you. I need you, Lizzie. You've changed me, made me unrecognisable to myself, and I need you to help me understand the person I've become. I need you to show me how to be the man you want me to be. I grew up without learning what love is. I need your help so that I can understand it. You humble me, Lizzie—with everything that you are.'

Could she believe him? Dared she?

He was going to lose her. In his pocket he could feel her wedding ring, the diamond of her engagement ring. Impulsively he dropped down on one knee in front of Lizzie, and removed the rings from his pocket.

'Please wear these again for me, Lizzie—for me, and our child, and the other children I want us to have. Be my wife and my love. I need you, Lizzie. I love you.'

Lizzie reached out and touched the dark head, her love for him filling her.

'There's nothing I wouldn't give up to have your love, Lizzie, not even Villa Manos. You've taught me that love matters more than anything else.'

'You'd give up your inheritance? But it's a sacred trust.'

'I won't sacrifice my love or my children for bricks and mortar.'

Now she believed him. Now she knew that he loved her and the child they were to have.

'Oh, Ilios.'

She was in his arms, and he was kissing her with a fierce need that told her more than words just how he really felt about her.

'I couldn't have let you go,' he told her emotionally. 'My life is nothing without you to share it with me, Lizzie.'

'Nor mine without you,' Lizzie whispered back to him lovingly.

'Don't look at me like that,' Ilios begged her. 'Not until we get home and I can show you how very much I want you.'

'Home. What a lovely word that is,' Lizzie told him. '*You* are our home, Ilios—mine and our baby's. Nothing else and no one else matters.'

The look of devotion and love on his face was everything her loving heart had longed to see there—and more.

0310/01/MB270

millsandboon.co.uk Community

Join Us!

The Community is the perfect place to meet and chat to kindred spirits who love books and reading as much as you do, but it's also the place to:

- Get the inside scoop from authors about their latest books
- Learn how to write a romance book with advice from our editors
- Help us to continue publishing the best in women's fiction
- Share your thoughts on the books we publish
- Befriend other users

Forums: Interact with each other as well as authors, editors and a whole host of other users worldwide.

Blogs: Every registered community member has their own blog to tell the world what they're up to and what's on their mind.

Book Challenge: We're aiming to read 5,000 books and have joined forces with The Reading Agency in our inaugural Book Challenge.

Profile Page: Showcase yourself and keep a record of your recent community activity.

Social Networking: We've added buttons at the end of every post to share via digg, Facebook, Google, Yahoo, technorati and de.licio.us.

www.millsandboon.co.uk

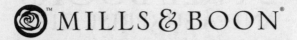

2 FREE BOOKS
AND A SURPRISE GIFT

We would like to take this opportunity to thank you for reading this Mills & Boon® book by offering you the chance to take TWO more specially selected books from the Modern™ series absolutely FREE! We're also making this offer to introduce you to the benefits of the Mills & Boon® Book Club™—

- **FREE home delivery**
- **FREE gifts and competitions**
- **FREE monthly Newsletter**
- **Exclusive Mills & Boon Book Club offers**
- **Books available before they're in the shops**

Accepting these FREE books and gift places you under no obligation to buy, you may cancel at any time, even after receiving your free books. Simply complete your details below and return the entire page to the address below. You don't even need a stamp!

YES Please send me 2 free Modern books and a surprise gift. I understand that unless you hear from me, I will receive 4 superb new books every month for just £3.19 each, postage and packing free. I am under no obligation to purchase any books and may cancel my subscription at any time. The free books and gift will be mine to keep in any case.

Ms/Mrs/Miss/Mr_____ Initials _____

Surname _____

Address _____

_____

_____ Postcode _____

Send this whole page to: Mills & Boon Book Club, Free Book Offer, FREEPOST NAT 10298, Richmond, TW9 1BR